THE RETURN OF MERLIN: EMRYS SERIES TWO
THE RETURN OF KING ARTHUR AND MORGANA PENDRAGON

RICHARD BERNARD

Copyright Notice

© 2024 by Richard Bernard. All rights reserved.

No part of this book, "**The Return of Merlin: Emrys with its subtitle as The Return of King Arthur and Morgana Pendragon**," may be reproduced, stored in a retrieval system, or transmitted in any form or by any means: electronic, mechanical, photocopying, recording, or otherwise without prior written permission from the copyright owner, except for brief quotations applied in critical reviews and certain other non-commercial uses permitted by copyright law.

This book is protected by copyright laws and international treaties. Unauthorized reproduction or distribution of this work, or any portion thereof, may result in severe civil and criminal penalties and will be prosecuted to the maximum extent permitted by law.

Contents

- COPYRIGHT NOTICE 2
- CHAPTER ONE 4
- HEROS' RETURN FROM THE DRAGON'S BATTLE 4
- CHAPTER TWO 10
- PRINCE ARTHUR'S TROUBLES 10
- CHAPTER THREE 23
- THE KING'S SWORD RELEASED FROM ROCK TO THRONE 23
- CHAPTER FOUR 57
- THE WONDERS OF PRINCE ARTHUR'S SWORD AS 'THE KINGS' SWORD' BEARER 57
- CHAPTER FIVE 80
- PRINCE ARTHUR'S DEADLY ENCOUNTER WITH THE FEARLESS ASSASSIN 80
- CHAPTER SIX 93
- THE KINGS' SWORD DISAPPEARANCE: THE TRIALS OF THE SWORD'S THIEF 93
- CHAPTER SEVEN 105
- THE NIGHT FOR NIGHTJAR'S EVIL MISSION 105

CHAPTER ONE

HEROS' RETURN FROM THE DRAGON'S BATTLE

The soldiers of Albion returned victoriously to Camelot from the dragon battle. As the knights and their foot soldiers approached the castle gates, the people of Camelot welcomed their heroes in style. Men, women, and children on top of the castle walls poured tiny, colorful pieces of paper (confetti) and leaves to celebrate their heroes.

A picture showing the triumphant return of Albion soldiers to Camelot after a victorious battle against Morgana's scary dragons.

Sir Percival, Sir Leon, and their fellow knights rode towards the castle, waving at the cheering crowd that had gathered to welcome them. According to Camelot's tradition, the King or Queen and the Royal Council must meet their heroes at the castle's gate. Thus, Queen Gwen Pendragon and her Royal Council were going downstairs to welcome the war heroes when they heard a loud sound. Young Arthur had just fallen off the chair while watching the soldiers enter the castle gate from the palace window.

Arthur was waving his hands just like the other citizens of Camelot, but he immediately fell when he set his eyes on Emrys, who was riding with the other knights. This is because he began to remember that he was once a king and that Emrys had been his closest ally, fighting by his side. As Emrys waved at the crowd in slow motion, his magical powers drew his attention to a particular lad at one of the palace windows, waving back. Both Emrys and Arthur's magical powers collided, and Arthur lost his balance and fell off the chair, catching Queen Gwen Pendragon's attention to her son.

Queen Gwen Pendragon asked, "Are you hurt?" Arthur replied, "No, I just want to go outside to see the men on horses." Gaius interjected, "There is nothing wrong with Prince Arthur joining the

Queen's entourage. After all, at eight years old, he should start learning the customs of Camelot." Queen Gwen declared to little Prince Arthur, "You'll join us in welcoming our heroes, but you must promise never to climb chairs and tables next time. You could hurt yourself." Prince Arthur nodded in response to his mother's request.

The people of Camelot remained silent, listening to the Queen's speech regarding their heroes' welcome. The Knights and their foot soldiers were already stationed at the palace gate when Queen Gwen Pendragon and her Royal Council arrived.

Queen Gwen Pendragon gave her speech. Today, we stand here, happy and proud because we have won a great battle. Our hearts still race with excitement, and we feel amazing because we were brave. We fought Morgana's terrifying dragons and emerged victorious, showing our strength and determination.

Remember, my friends, that Camelot's strength isn't just about our swords and armor. It's about the strong spirit inside us, a spirit that never gives up, no matter how hard things get.

Even when things looked dark, we believed in ourselves and in each other. We faced every danger that came our way, knowing it wouldn't be easy. We never gave up because we wanted Camelot to be safe and peaceful.

Today, as we celebrate our victory, let's remember those who fought with us. They were brave, and their courage kept us going, no matter what. We are the protectors of Camelot, and as long as we stay brave and kind, no bad thing can ever beat us.

So, let's hold our swords up high and cheer loudly. Today, we've shown that nothing can defeat the strong spirit of Camelot! The people of Camelot cheered, "Long live the Queen!"

Meanwhile, as Queen Gwen Pendragon was giving her speech, Emrys stood amidst the cheering crowd, his eyes scanning the faces of the jubilant citizens of Camelot. He couldn't help but feel a surge of pride. Emrys raised his hand in a regal wave, acknowledging the people's adoration. But little did he know that his magical powers were at play, drawing him to a particular lad in the crowd.

Unbeknownst to Emrys, that lad happened to be none other than the mischievous Prince Arthur, whose reborn essence was brimming with magical potential, much like Merlin himself. As their powers collided, chaos ensued, much to Emrys' dismay and Arthur's delight.

Arthur could even talk directly to Emrys, just like Mordred when he was a lad like Arthur. Arthur said, "Hello, Emrys, we meet again." Emrys replied, "How did you know my name?" "I not only know your name but also recognize your abilities and purpose in Camelot. I remember you were an ally to Camelot during my reign as king." Replied Arthur. Emrys was surprised at Arthur's magical memory abilities. Emrys quickly recovered from shock as the loud cheers for the Queen's speech interrupted his conversation with Arthur.

Emrys experienced magical manipulations from the young Prince Arthur, which were unknown to anyone except Emrys and Arthur. Arthur wanted to continue his friendship with Emrys and, therefore, decided to suffer Emrys with some magical tricks during the Queen's speech. Queen Gwen Pendragon looked at Emrys and said, 'I love your display of magic to my people and your great assistance.' Gaius looked at Emrys, wondering why he would display magical tricks during the Queen's important speech. After delivering her speech, Queen Gwen Pendragon and her entourage returned to the castle.

CHAPTER TWO

PRINCE ARTHUR'S TROUBLES

Arthur remembered that Emrys had been a friend of Camelot before his death. Arthur saw visions of his past life with Emrys, especially how Emrys protected his soldiers from Morgana Pendragon's dragon, which rained fire on his soldiers. In Arthur's visions, Emrys uses his firing eyes and magical words to drive off the dragon in order to protect him and his Knights when Arthur leads his men to war as King of Camelot. Thus, these visions made Arthur want to reconnect with Emrys, hoping to rekindle their friendship as in the old days before his death. Arthur decided to search for Emrys, suspecting that he might be staying in one of the castle's rooms as a guest. Emrys had already transformed into Merlin and was in his place with Gaius in their quarter in the castle.

Eventually, one of the rooms that Arthur visited happened to be Merlin and Gaius's room. Just before Arthurs arrives at Merlin and Gaius's place, Gaius asks Merlin suspiciously, "Why're you wandering around the room?" Merlin replied Gaius, "I was nearly humiliated by Prince Arthur in front of the Queen and Knights today.

Firstly, Arthur started playing pranks on me. He made my hat disappear and reappear, and I couldn't do anything to stop it. Therefore, making Camelot's great sorcerer scratched his head in confusion. Then, with a flick of Arthur's wrist, he caused my beard to grow wildly out of control. Thus, this made me the source of amusement for the people of Camelot. Gaius started laughing at Merlin.

But Arthur wasn't done yet. With a mischievous grin, Arthur turned my staff into a real chicken that you saw me holding that time. Arthur's magic had me, an eighty-year-old wizard, flailing about in an attempt to catch the running chicken so that I could change the chicken back to its original form. Gaius continues to laugh at Merlin's words.

Merlin wasn't moved by Gaius laughing as he was still complaining. Despite my best efforts to regain control of the situation, Arthur's antics continued unabated. Arthur changed my robes to neon pink and transformed my voice into a chorus of squeaks and squawks, and he was the one that conjured a swarm of butterflies to flutter around my bewildered wizard's head.

Throughout the Queen's speech, I couldn't do anything but sputter in disbelief. I couldn't control Arthur's magic tricks because my magical attempts failed. I could only join in the merriment, waiting for the Queen's speech to end.

Gaius holds Merlin's shoulder to comfort him. Gaius said, "Merlin, in the end, the crowd erupted into laughter at the spectacle unfolding before them. No one eventually knew what really happened between you and Arthur. I believe the people of Camelot appreciated Arthur's pranks, especially because they came from the unlikeliest person—a mischievous young Prince Arthur."

Suddenly, there came a knock at the door. "Let me get the door, " said Gaius. "Hi, sir, can I come in?" Requested Arthur, who was standing at the door. Merlin guessed within his mind whose voice it was at the door, pleading to come in. Merlin guesses within his mind about whose person's voice it was at the door pleading to come in.

Merlin could feel the same presence of Arthur's magical powers just like when he was coming with the Knight. Merlin says to himself, "This means Arthur's troubles have finally entered his room."

Gaius couldn't respond to Prince Arthur because he was surprised to see the person, they were discussing in front of him and standing at his door after opening it. More surprisingly, Gaius was suspicious that Arthur might recognize him and Merlin.

"Sir, may I come in," asks Prince Arthur the second time, looking at Gaius for a response. "My apologies, my Prince. Yes, yes, you're free to come in." Answer Gaius. Gaius continues, "I was shocked to see you (Prince Arthur) standing at my door."

"How can I be of help to you, my Lordship?" Asked Gaius. "I'm searching for a friend." Replied Prince Arthur. Gaius said, "I was wondering how you know my name. What is the name of the friend you're searching for?" "My friend's name is Emrys. Something tells me that you're Gaius, and Merlin is the person standing beside you." Replied Prince Arthur.

Merlin interrupts Arthur, "Before you died, you knew all of us as your friends. Why are you pretending now that you didn't know us after returning from the dead?" Just as Prince Arthur wanted to respond to Merlin's observation about Arthur returning from the dead and pretending not to know them, a knock suddenly came at the door. A soldier asked without waiting for a response from anybody, "Is the Prince at your place?" Gaius replied, "Yes, I suppose he was wandering around the castle and entered our quarters by mistake."

Then the soldier shouted to his commander, "The Prince is here!" Merlin, Gaius, and Prince Arthur could hear the rushing of soldiers' feet towards their room. The captain of the Queen's guard stood at Gaius's door and said, "My Prince, the Queen requests your immediate attention in her quarters!" Arthur told Merlin and Gaius, "I'll see you again, my old friends." Prince Arthur then opens the door, and the Queen's guards follow Arthur to the Queen's quarters.

Merlin sat down and said to Gaius, "My greatest fear is that how could Prince Arthur stop me from using my magical powers to defend myself from Arthur's magic pranks." Gaius said to Merlin while holding Merlin's hands to comfort him, "let's wait and see how things unfold. I'm sure Arthur's return from the dead is for good and not for evil. You didn't have to worry much. Let find something to eat before night falls."

At night, Arthur could not sleep after searching for Emrys for a long time without finding him. He decided to talk to Emrys, just as he had when Arthur saw Emrys returning with the soldiers. Prince Arthur called out to Emrys (using a magical voice similar to a druid's communication), "My friend, are you still at Camelot?" Merlin was asleep when he heard Prince Arthur's voice. Merlin fell off his bed because he knew Arthur was about to cause more trouble, just as he had publicly that morning. "I just want to say hello."

Prince Arthur said. Merlin, who was the same old man as Emrys, didn't want to reply to Arthur's callings. Prince Arthur continued calling, "Emrys! Emrys! Please answer me."

Unbeknownst to Emrys and Arthur, Morgana Pendragon overheard Prince Arthur calling out to Emrys in the druid way. Arthur's yelling for Emrys' attention woke Morgana in her castle at the Isle of the Blessed. Morgana Pendragon could hear Prince Arthur and Emrys' discussions because the presence of the evil power at the Isle of the Blessed kept increasing her powers. " This time, I will do everything in my power to end your life, little brother, and that of your friend, Emrys. I must get the magical vessel containing the wizards' and witches' souls at all cost so that I can draw more powers in order to kill all my enemies." Morgana Pendragon said to herself.

Merlin decides to reply to Prince Arthur's callings. Merlin transformed himself into Emrys so as to respond in Emrys' voice. Emrys replied to Arthur, "Yes, I'm in Camelot." "That is great! Where exactly are you staying?" Asked Arthur happily. "In one of the rooms in your castle." Replied Emrys. "Which room exactly are you staying in? I want us to play magical tricks together again." Begged Arthur. Emrys said, "No!" Magic tricks are forbidden in Camelot. Besides, it is night. I would never allow you to play magical tricks on me."

Arthur replied to Emrys, "Okay, can we play in the morning?" Merlin protested to Arthur angrily, saying: "magic tricks aren't permitted in Camelot. Therefore, I will never allow you to use your magic on me again." Arthur said, 'I'm sorry." Arthur pleads, saying, "Don't worry, we can secretly play magic in your room or quarters. I would search for you in all the rooms in the castle in the morning again." Emrys said to himself: "Arthur's troubles will be the death of me one day. He won't let me rest or sleep." Emrys sleeps off after hearing Arthur's intention of searching for him again in the morning.

In the morning, Gaius was surprised to find Merlin still asleep and transformed into Emrys. Gaius said: "Wake up, Emrys! You must transform back into Merlin before anyone sees you." Emrys quickly transformed back into Merlin. Merlin told Gaius, "While you were snoring last night, Prince Arthur begged me to play magical tricks with him. I could hear him calling my name, "Emrys, Emrys," over and over. Thus, I had to transform into Emrys to answer him. I've to do that in order to prevent one with similar powers like ours from discovering Arthur's magical abilities."

Gaius said happily, "One thing is certain: Arthur hasn't figured out who you truly are. I mean, he doesn't know you're the Emrys he's been searching for." Merlin asked Gaius, "Are you sure?" Gaius nodded to Merlin, "Yes, the fact that Arthur was calling out 'Emrys' without knowing which room you were in proves he doesn't recognize you as Emrys." Merlin stood up from his bed and walked around the room. Merlin replied to Gaius, "Arthur never called me 'Emrys' the last time he came to our room. Arthur called me, Merlin,' You might be right." Gaius continued, 'There is only one way to find out, Merlin: if Arthur comes here again and calls you Merlin without saying Emrys."

The next day, as the morning sun cast its golden rays upon the castle of Camelot, Merlin awoke to the sound of birds chirping outside his window. Little did he know, another day of mischief awaited him, courtesy of the ever-curious Prince Arthur. It begins just after Gaius and Merlin have had breakfast when they hear the warning bell. The soldiers were once again searching for Prince Arthur. Gaius and Merlin went outside to inquire about the reason for the warning bell. One of the Queen's guards told them that Prince Arthur was missing. Merlin told Gaius, "This means another day of troublemaking. Remember Prince Arthur told me he would be searching the whole castle for Emrys? He'll surely come off his search for Emrys whenever he is tired of looking for him."

Merlin then went into his room while Gaius followed him. Gaius told Merlin, "I think you're wrong. Maybe Morgana Pendragon kidnapped Prince Arthur, contrary to what you're insinuating. Remember you told me that someone with special powers like Morgana Pendragon could hear him calling you." Merlin asked Gaius, "Why is Prince Arthur such a troublesome lad?" Gaius replied to Merlin, "That is the wrong question; the right question should be where the Prince is?" "There is only one solution for finding Prince Arthur. Answer Merlin. "Then what is the solution for finding Prince Arthur." Asked Gaius. Merlin says to Gaius, "He wants me to play with him. If I tell Prince Arthur to come out of his hiding place, then I must promise to play magic with him." Gaius sat down and said, "That is true. It is the only way to stop the present chaos caused by this troublesome lad." Merlin said, "Talking to him will also reveal Prince Arthur's whereabouts. He has put us in a position where we have no choice but to fulfill his request to find Emrys." Merlin continues, "I've to become his playmate in order to stop this mad search." "Then what are we going to do now, Merlin?" Asked Gaius. "I'll have to do what I hate doing. I'll transform into Emrys and call Arthur in the spiritual world." Said Merlin.

Merlin recited some magical words, and he

transformed into Emrys. "Hello, Prince Arthur, where are you?" Asked Emrys. "Emrys! Emrys!! Is that you?" Asked Prince Arthur. "Yes, where are you?" Asked Emrys. "I'm hiding under my mother's bed. Since you don't want to play with me. I decide to remain lonely." Replied Prince Arthur. "Ok, I'll play with you if you come out and ask for permission from the Queen to play with me. You must also promise me not do this again, then we will be friends. I'll only play magical tricks with you for only today. This will be our last magic play time. Then I will leave Camelot. I'll be in Gaius and Merlin's room waiting for you." Replied Merlin. Prince Arthur promised Merlin to keep his word.

"Who could that be at this hour?" Emrys muttered to himself as he made his way to the door. To his surprise, standing on the other side was none other than Prince Arthur, his face alight with excitement and mischief. "Good morning, Emrys! I'm ready for another day of magical adventures!" Arthur exclaimed, his eyes gleaming with mischief.

Merlin's heart sank as he realized that Arthur was intent on causing trouble again. But before he could protest, Arthur had already barged into the room, his eyes darting around eagerly in search of hidden wonders. "Emrys, my friend, I've come to play magical tricks with you!" Arthur declared, his voice ringing with enthusiasm. Merlin, still disguised as Emrys, could only sigh in resignation. No amount of pleading or reasoning seemed to dissuade the determined Prince from his mischief.

A picture of Prince Arthur playing magical tricks with Merlin (disguised as Emrys).

"Arthur, I told you before: magic tricks are forbidden in Camelot," Emrys replied, trying his best to caution Prince Arthur. "Besides, it's far too early for such nonsense. Can't we just enjoy a quiet morning for once?" However, Arthur was undeterred, his eyes sparkling with mischief as he scanned the room for hidden treasures. "Come on, Emrys, don't be such a stick in the mud! I know you've hidden some magical secrets in this room, and I intend to find them!" Arthur exclaimed, his enthusiasm undiminished.

With that, Arthur set to work, rummaging through Emrys's belongings with the zeal of a treasure hunter on a quest. Arthur overturned cushions, rifled through drawers, and even climbed onto chairs in search of hidden wonders. Emrys could only watch in dismay as Arthur wreaked havoc upon his neatly organized room, his protests falling on deaf ears. "Arthur, please, you're making a mess!" Emrys cried, trying in vain to restore order to the chaos that had erupted around him. But Arthur paid him no mind, his determination unshakeable as he continued his search for magical treasures. Finally, after what felt like hours of chaos, Arthur let out a triumphant cry upon discovering a dusty old tome hidden beneath a pile of blankets.

"Eureka!" Arthur exclaimed, holding the ancient

book aloft. "I knew there had to be something magical hidden away in this room!" Emrys, resigned to his fate, could only shake his head in exasperation as Arthur began to leafed through the pages of the ancient tome, his eyes shining with excitement.

CHAPTER THREE

THE KING'S SWORD RELEASED FROM ROCK TO THRONE

Gaius came back to find Merlin (Emrys) in a deep sleep. He assumed it was due to Arthur's troubles caused by his attempts to play magical tricks with Emrys. Gaius locked the door to prevent anyone from discovering Emrys's true identity. Gaius also wanted to cover Emrys with a cloth to prevent him from getting cold, but suddenly, he saw a ball appearing on Emrys' right hand. The ball rested on Emrys' right hand. It seemed like a glowing ball that appeared on Merlin's hand during the days of Nimueh. Nimueh, the sorceress who once poisoned Merlin. Also, the ball resembled transparent glass, appearing to display Emrys's (Merlin's) dreams at that moment. With his vast magical knowledge of the Old Religion, Gaius understood the mysteries surrounding Emrys and the transparent ball, interpreting it as a message from a deceased person meant for Emrys.

A picture of Emrys (Merlin) holding a ball, which looks like a transparent glass. The ball shows Emrys' dreams about 'The Kings' Sword' and the Swordbearer.

Gaius hid in a corner of the room while viewing and listening to the dead person's messages to Emrys. This is because the dead person could see Gaius through the ball in Emrys's hand. This could prompt the messenger to stop talking to Emrys immediately upon noticing that another person is listening to the message.

Gaius could see wars between Kingdoms fighting for the sword inside the ball on Merlin's hand as the narrator (Balinor) was talking to Merlin. Thousands of wounded and dead soldiers scattered everywhere on the battlefield because of "The Kings' Sword". Gaius also saw battles among wizards and witches, each fighting for this particular sword. Any wizards or witches who become the sword's keeper would be powerful and respectful throughout the world. All of these happened because of the sword.

Balinor appears on the transparent ball and calls Merlin (Emrys), saying, "My son, I'm glad that you've taken my place as a wise and good wizard. I'm also happy that Kings respect you for your courage for good and not for evil. Please forgive me, my son, for not spending as much time with you as a father should. I must share something with you that I should have told you while I was alive. Something that I can call a family secret. Something your great grandfather (Ardgal, who was our ancestral legend) told my grandfather (Dragomir) before he died. Something that had to do with the 'Kings' Sword.' Sometimes, during the height of the old religion, there used to be a magical sword that any King or Kingdom desired to possess. The Kings' Sword happened to be one of Albion's greatest untold secrets, which was driven into a rock. Merlin, your late great grandfather (Dragomir), had driven a powerful sword into a mountain close to Emperor Constantine's palace (the late Uther Pendragon's grandfather). He struck the sword into the rock so that the sword would be in Albion. It was Constantine's turn to wheel the sword. The sword was the most powerful instrument of war ever wielded by any King who had ruled over Camelot and beyond. The sword was powerful because it granted magical skill and exceptional swordsmanship to anyone who wielded it.

The picture of 'The Kings' Sword' driven into the rock by Dragomir.

Interestingly, it is believed that any swordsperson who happens to remove the sword will automatically rule over Camelot and the other Kingdoms forever. Additionally, the Kings' Sword brings economic prosperity to any kingdom that possesses it. Prophecies foretell that the land where the sword rests will be blessed with riches. Surely, Camelot's riches and wealth were a result of the sword's resting place, which happened to be on a mountain close to the King's palace during the era of the great Emperor Constantine. Kingdoms united against Albion in attempts to retrieve the irremovable sword from the rock in order to gain possession of this great legendary sword. Their failure was believed to be because of the sword's resting place in Camelot. The sword is a symbol of magical defense for any Kingdom, where it is the resting place of the great sword. All these prompted many great kings to send witches and wizards to retrieve the sword from the rock. Unfortunately, no mortal has successfully retrieved the sword from the rock where it was buried. However, none of them could remove the sword from the rock except the person who buried the sword in the rock or any of his powerful descendants, who also must be powerful like the original person who buried the sword. At this time, Emrys (Merlin) is the only rightful person with the qualities needed to remove the sword.

You're Dragomir's great-grandson. Dragomir buried the sword to prevent anyone from using the powers in the sword for evil, which is the reason why many knights failed to remove the sword from its resting place.

Dragomir, who was also my grandfather, held the titles: 'The Kings' Sword Keeper' and 'The Dragon Lord.' He was the one who discovered that it was the Pendragon's turn to wheel the sword. He sent Constantine (the late King Uther Pendragon's grandfather) a message. The sword was deemed fit for the household of the Pendragons. Constantine was very happy to receive such good news that any King would ever dream of the sword. Constantine prepares the most enormous and colorful banquet for the coming keeper of the Kings' Sword. Your grandfather arrived at the banquet and was very entertained. He was about to bless Constantine with the sword when Arthwys Pendragon (late King Uther's Pendragon father) entered into the banquet. Arthwys wasn't around but with Constantine's soldiers at a faraway land when he got the news about the sword and decided to join his father in celebrating the sword ownership.

When the announcer announced the entrance of Arthwys Pendragon into the banquet, Dragomir looked into his eyes. He could see the vision of terrible killings and destructions that would eventually take place during the reign of Arthwys' Pendragon, heir to the throne. He fed the banquet and was being chased by soldiers on the order of Arthwys Pendragon. Many arrows from Arthwys' men struck him. He then deep half the length of 'The Kings' Sword' into the mountain near Constantine's palace. He caused that no man would ever remove the sword from the rock except him or his descendants. The great dragon came to rescue him. Before Balinor died, he entrusted the secrets of the Kings' Sword to me. King Uther Pendragon wasn't after me because of just being the 'Dragon Lord' only; he was also after my life for being the 'Kings' Sword Keeper.'" This was why I was King Uther Pendragon's most wanted man. The late King Arthwys Pendragon must have given those instructions to King Uther Pendragon before he died. Thus, this was one of the reasons why the late King Uther Pendragon hated magical people like us more than his late father (King Arthwys Pendragon).

The late King Arthwys and Uther Pendragon wanted a revenge on Dragomir for making the late King Constantine sad for the rest of his life.

The picture of the late King Constantine is of him looking unhappy for the rest of his life for not being able to wheel 'The Kings' Sword' even when he was entitled to it as the Swordbearer.

My son, the main reason for talking to you is that the rightful person to wield the Kings' Sword has been born into the Pendragon line. He is none other than Prince Arthur. Prince Arthur is someone who isn't afraid of magic and a direct descendant of the Pendragon lineage. You're assigned another role as the Kings' Sword Keeper to Prince Arthur. As the old dragon (Kilgharrah) had told you, you're to mentor Prince Arthur so that he could be a successful wielder of the Kings' Sword. I will always be with you, my son. Ask the old dragon whenever you want to talk to me about the Kings' Sword, and Kilgharrah will tell you what to do. Goodbye, my son.

Immediately, the glowing and transparent ball on Emrys' right hand disappeared, and Emrys woke up, shouting Arthur! Arthur!! Gaius realizes that Balinor's messages to Merlin have ended and decides to comfort Emrys because he was confused. Gaius said, "Emrys, it's over; stop shouting. You've just had a dream. You must transform into Merlin before someone in the castle discovers your true identity. It was morning already, and people in the castle would start waking up from bed."

Emrys transformed into his true self (Merlin) and sat on a chair. Gaius also sat next to him. Merlin couldn't say a word for almost an hour. He was just holding his head. Gaius realizes the shock that Merlin went through and decides to talk things out.

"Why are you still holding your head for so long?" Asked Gaius. "It is because of that troublesome Prince Arthur." Merlin replied. Gaius said, "No, I guess that isn't why." Merlin asked Gaius, "Why did you say so?" Gaius replies, " The reason is that Prince Arthur has become the wielder of the Kings' Sword, and he is the first troublesome wielder you've ever encountered." Merlin asked Gaius, "How did you know this?" Gaius said, "Merlin, I heard everything your father told you. I saw the magical ball in your hand. I know that Prince Arthur would change one day because he can't continue to be a lad forever." Merlin replied Gaius, "You're right, he would change. I just have to endure his troubles." Said Merlin. Merlin continues, "The problem is that I see nothing important about the Kings' Sword. The sword's resting place has become a place where an old sword got stuck in a rock and not much people know about the sword's tales." Gaius said, "It would be crazy telling a troublesome Prince Arthur about the Kings' Sword at this time. I suggest you ask the old dragon about what to do. Let me get something for us to eat."

Merlin took his medicine bags as if he was going

to fetch herbals and went far into the woods. He calls on the old dragon. The old dragon traveled to meet Merlin in the forest. Merlin told the old dragon, "What am I going to do now that I'm the Kings' Sword Keeper to a troublesome Prince?" Kilgharrah (old dragon) said, "The magic behind the Kings' Sword is too powerful for me to understand. All I would know is that the Kings' Sword would find its wielder when the time comes. Just as your father told you, Merlin, you mustn't be too far from the Prince. Merlin, you must mentor Prince Arthur to become a successful King. You must exercise patience and endurance with Prince Arthur. I'm sure he wouldn't be trouble forever."

A picture of Kilgharrah (the old dragon) speaking to Merlin about Merlin's role as the Keeper of the Kings' Sword and his duty to guide Prince Arthur in the woods.

Merlin said, "You mean that the Kings' Sword would find its wielder by itself?" "Yes, replied the old dragon." Merlin returned home and told Gaius about what the old dragon had told him. Gaius and Merlin waited for the day that the Kings' Sword would locate its wielder by itself.

Everyone in Camelot woke up in the mid-morning to the ringing emergency bell on the seventh day after Merlin received a message from his father (Balinor). The bell also woke Queen Gwen and all the Knights, as well as Merlin and Gaius. Unlike any other time, the bell wasn't ringing because Prince Arthur went missing, but something strange had just happened. Everyone in Camelot opened their windows and doors because the forsaken sword in the rock had started shining. Half the size of the Kings' Sword (as it's known) has shone like the sun even though the sun has not risen yet.

Gaius told Merlin, "I guess the shining of the Kings' Sword is calling its bearer. I want to go to bed because I know the Queen will summon an emergency meeting in the morning." Gaius went to bed, leaving Merlin to gaze at the shining sword from their window. Just after having their breakfast, Merlin and Gaius received a message from the Queen's guard that there was an emergency meeting at the Queen's court.

Unlike before, the attendance at the Queen's court was complete. Everyone was present, murmuring among themselves about why the forsaken old sword had started to shine. Sir Leon approached Gaius and asked, "Before the Queen arrives, do you have anything to say about the shining sword?" All the Knights look up to Gaius because they know he is the first person among them to talk about Morgana Pendragon's resurrection from the dead. Therefore, they knew that Gaius had answers to most of the problems that Camelot was facing. As Gaius was about to respond to Sir Leon's request, the Queen's arrival announcement was made by a colorful announcer dressed in native Camelot customs.

All the Queen's court members took their seats after the Queen sat on her throne. Queen Gwen asked her court, "Does anyone know why the old sword is shining?" Everybody was speechless. No one was bold enough to provide a complete explanation for why the old stuck sword had begun to shine at this moment. All the court members looked at Gaius because they knew he always had great wisdom concerning incidents such as this particular one. But there wasn't a response from Gaius himself because he could discuss Merlin's family secrets in the Queen's court.

Suddenly, Geoffrey of Monmouth, who is the chief librarian, stood up and said, "I guessed I might know the reason why the old stuck sword is shining." Everyone looked at Geoffrey with great expectations except Gaius. Gaius was relieved from the physiological troubles going on in his mind, such as whether or not to disclose the Kings' Sword secrets to the Queen's court.

Geoffrey (the chief librarian) stood up and said, "The sword stuck in the rock is known as The Kings' Sword, according to legend. It is said to belong to all great Kings, but only one King can claim it, which is why it is called The Kings' Sword.".

The Kings' Sword is said to bring unimaginable economic prosperity to Albion. Additionally, any King who wields The Kings' Sword would become invincible in battle. According to the King's records in my possession, the event leading to the sword being stuck into a rock happened long ago during the time of King Constantine (late King Uther Pendragon's grandfather) and his son, the late King Arthwys Pendragon (King Uther Pendragon's father). The late King Constantine was a close friend of Dragomir, who was the 'Dragon Lord' and Keeper of 'The Kings' Sword' at the same time. Unfortunately, Dragomir wasn't friendly with the late King Constantine's son, who happened to be the late King Arthwys Pendragon. According to the Kings' historical records with me, Dragomir was afraid of how late King Arthwys would wield the sword during his reign. Therefore, Dragomir drove 'The Kings' Sword' into the rock while being pursued by King Arthwys' men."

Sir Geraint stood up and said, "The mysteries of 'The Kings' Sword' are old and have become a myth except for the fact that the sword started shining recently. All the people you mentioned are dead, and there is actually no one except historical records bearing witness to the Kings' Sword legend." Geoffrey said, " Not everyone from that time has passed away. There is one man who was cursed to witness 'The Kings' Sword's bearer' before his death." He was to bear testimony to the events that happened until The Kings' Sword wielder emerged. He is the only person who became untouchable by the late Kings Arthwys and Uther Pendragon because he cannot be killed by any human or by any magical power. His name is Galador. Galador is presently the oldest man living man of our time because he is still expecting to see 'The Kings' Sword wielder before he dies." Geoffrey continues, "Galador lives closer to the resting place of 'The Kings' Sword' because seeing the sword prolongs his life."

Queen Gwen rose from her throne and ordered Sir

Leon and Sir Percival to find Galador so that he could and testify before the Royal Court about the Kings' Sword. Queen Gwen told the Royal Court to keep today's meeting a secret until the arrival of Galador. The Queen took her leave so that the Knights could prepare to find Galador.

Sir Leon couldn't ask Gaius about the Kings' Sword since he had been assigned an important task to locate the whereabouts of Galador. Therefore, Gaius and Merlin return to their quarters in the castle. Merlin told Gaius, "I don't know how the Queen will react when she learns that the new 'The Kings' Swordbearer happens to be her son."

The next day, there was a knock on Gaius and Merlin's door. Gaius opened and wasn't surprised to see Prince Arthur, escorted by two royal guards at the door because he was now used to his frequent visits. "You may come in, my Lordship." Gaius requested Prince Arthur. "What brings you here my Prince?" Merlin asked Prince Arthur as he placed a chair for him to sit on. "I just wanted to ask Emrys some questions because I haven't been able to sleep since the mountain sword began to shine." Replying to Merlin's request. Merlin and Gaius looked at each other because they were surprised at Arthur's response. Merlin continues questioning Prince Arthur, "We're

Emrys' friends. Can you explain what you meant when you said you couldn't sleep since the day 'The Kings' Sword' started shining?'" Thus, Prince Arthur answered Merlin, saying, "That sword you called 'The Kings' Sword' has been calling my name since it started shining." Gaius asked Prince Arthur, "Have you told anyone about this?" "No, I haven't told anyone except you and Merlin because we're friends." Replied Prince Arthur. Prince Arthur continues, "The Queen has ordered the royal guards not to allow me to leave her quarter except if I want to visit Gaius and Merlin's quarters. Thus, I couldn't visit the resting place of 'The Kings' Sword' as ordinary people do. I can view the sword through my window. What is troubling more is that the shining sword kept calling my name. The sword calls my name everyday since it started shinning on the rock."

Merlin, Gaius, and Prince Arthur looked out of the window. From upstairs, they saw many people from across Albion entering Camelot to see the shining sword driven into the mountain. "So many people entering Camelot to see the shining sword." Said Gaius. "Yes," Replied Queen Gwen behind them. Gaius said surprisingly, "My Queen, we didn't realize when you entered our room." Queen Gwen said happily, holding her son's hands, "I'm glad that my son finds your friendship befitting. There is going to be a short meeting today at the Queen's Court; please be there." Queen Gwen leaves with her son (Prince Arthur).

At the Queen's Court, everybody was present. There was silence this time because a strange old man accompanied by a young lad was in attendance for the first time. Queen Gwen entered the Royal Court, and everyone took their seats. Sir Leon and Percival stood up and Sir Leon said, "My Queen, I present the attendance of Galador to the Royal Court.

Galador was a very old man to behold. Galador's pale skin and his skin's whitish color exposed Galador's skeletal frame. Galador's old, aging body prevented his clothes from hanging properly on his body. Most of Galador's hair on his head had fallen off naturally due to continuing aging without dying. His voice had changed from deep and masculine to weak and fragile. Galador's sight (his eyes) are the only perfect part of his body so that he can see 'The Kings' Swordbearer clearly in fulfillment of the prophecy according to the legend of the sword. All these Galador's descriptions demonstrate Galador as a terrible old personality to behold.

Sir Leon told the Queen, "He is too old to speak. Galador would be assisted by an interpreter who happens to be his great-grandson." Queen Gwen granted an audience for Galador to speak. Galador stood up and started talking (something he had never done for many years due to his continuous aging without dying).

Queen Gwen interrupted Galador by saying, "My Knights told me that you couldn't speak well and stand up on your own; how come you could speak and stand all by yourself?" "I guessed 'The Kings' Swordbearer is very close because I haven't felt like this before. I strongly felt the presence of 'The Kings' Swordbearer in your court. I also felt the presence of Dragomir in this room. That is the reason why I could stand and speak clearly." Said Galador.

The only ones who got what Galador was saying about the Swordbearer being nearby were Gaius and Merlin. Galador continues his speech, "I was there when Dragomir got attacked by the late King Arthwys Pendragon (King Uther Pendragon's father). Dragomir was a good wizard. Dragomir was able to cure any ailment with his magical gifts. He didn't any money for his cures and medicines. Most good kings respected and honored him throughout Albion and other Kingdoms far away. Unlike most wizards, Dragomir wasn't selfish at all. He inherited two magical positions: 'The Dragon Lord' and 'The Keeper of the Kings' Sword' during his time. Unfortunately, Dragomir was hated by wicked

Kings and wizards. On the night he was attacked, I saw King Arthwys' men chasing him and, at the same time the soldiers were firing arrows at Dragomir from all directions. I knew he wouldn't last long before his capture. Therefore, I threw myself in the direction of the remaining arrows so that Dragomir could escape when he came closer to the door beside me. I was able to close the door so that Dragomir wouldn't be hit by any arrows intended for him. Before Dragomir left, he told me I wouldn't die until another 'Keeper of the Kings' Sword' showed up because he was surprised by what I did. I endured all the punishment done me to by the late two Kings, but none was able to kill me because the sword's magical powers continued to heal me each time the two Kings injured my body with their punishment. Eventually, I was banished from Albion but allow to visit the Kings' sword's resting place because of my nobility. I'm again I felt the presence of one of the descendants of Dragomir in our mist."

Queen Gwen asked Dragomir, "How old are you?" Dragomir replied to Queen Gwen, "I'm over 500 years old and won't die until I see the bearer of 'The Kings' Sword' with my own eyes."

Queen Gwen apologizes on behalf of the Pendragon's family. Queen announces the removal of the law, banishing Galador to stop immediately. She ordered the chief librarian (Geoffrey) to compensate Galador with a thousand gold coins, and Galador should be allowed to remain in Camelot. The Queen granted a royal membership title to Galador. There was clapping of hands to welcome a new member into the royal Council.

As all the members sat down after welcoming Galador into their mist, Sir Safer said, "He observed that more folks are pouring into Camelot to see the shining sword, and all the inns were now filled up. We need to increase taxes in order to generate more money from people visiting to see the shining sword. This would enable Camelot recover all the expenses spent on previous wars fought." All the Royal Council Members supported Sir Safer's idea. Sir Bedwere said, "He observed one unfortunate thing with 'The Kings' Sword' shining at this time, the buried sword in the rock has also become a place where gangsters bet for money to remove the sword."

Sir Bedwere's observation brought sadness into the mist of the Royal Council Members. Then Galador stood up and said, "The people are doing these things for one purpose, which is to find the Swordbearer." Sir Leon proposes an idea not to disturb the people betting on the removal of 'The Kings' Sword'; instead, the Council's attention should use it as a strategy to find the Swordbearer that is closer, just as Galador has said." Sir Safer suggested that the Queen tax the folks betting on the sword so no one gets suspicious that we're looking for the actual sword wielder.

Then Queen Gwen stood up and thanked all the members. She told the soldiers to dress up and act like gangsters while they waited for the rightful Swordbearer to show up at 'The Kings' Sword' resting place. Queen Gwen also ordered Sir Safer to collect taxes so that no one would suspect that they were after the Swordbearer. These strategies are secrets that the Royal Council Members must keep until 'The Kings' Sword Wielder' emerges. The royal meeting ended with these plans.

Gaius and Merlin returned to their quarters after a long meeting with the Queen. Merlin asked Gaius, "How would the Queen feel when she finally discovered that 'The Kings' Swordbearer' they are searching for is her son?"

All these times, the news of 'The Kings' Sword' spread far into many places. As a result, different people visited Camelot every day. The good thing is that the taxes collected from people entering Camelot brought great riches to Albion.

For a long stretch, Arthur's guards kept him stuck in the Queen's quarters. Besides the Queen's quarters, the guards didn't let Arthur let him set foot beyond Gaius and Merlin's quarters for over three months. Restrictively, Arthur's guards didn't let him go anywhere else in the castle nor allowed him to leave the castle as well.

Prince Arthur could only look at 'The Kings' Sword' from his window in the castle, especially when the sword started calling out to him. The Kings' Sword could only be heard by Prince Arthur. Sometimes, the calling made him stare at the sword day and night. Thus, Arthur's obsession with 'The Kings' Sword' sometimes worried Queen Gwen. Queen Gwen was so caught up with her royal duties that she let Arthur keep staring at 'The Kings' Sword' all the time. She thought that Arthur would eventually get tired of staring at the sword as he grew older.

One day, Arthur came up with the perfect plan to sneak off to 'The Kings' Sword's' resting place without anyone suspecting him or even catching on him. Arthur found an old suit of armor he used to wear when he was younger, back before he died. Arthur threw on the armor and snuck out of the castle without Queen Gwen or her guards noticing. When Arthur approached another exist surrounded by soldiers and royal guards, the soldiers and royal guards couldn't stop him or ask any question but to salute him because he had worn a Prince's armor.

Merlin and Gaius were on their way to give the Queen her medicine when they noticed the man in a Prince's armor vest leaving the Queen's quarters. Merlin leaned over and whispered into Gaius, saying, "Who could be this man in a Prince's armor?" "He might be an assassin here to kill the Queen or Prince Arthur," Gaius replied.

Arthur managed to slip out of the castle before Merlin and Gaius could alert Queen Gwen of the strange man in a Prince's armor vest leaving the castle.

The Queen asked the captain of the royal guards' captain about Prince Arthur's whereabouts. After searching for Arthur's whereabouts for over an hour, the captain of the royal guards returns, saying, "The Prince is missing."

Camelot's emergency bell started clanging to alert the Queen's guards and Knights. However, most of the Knights were at the resting place of 'The Kings' Sword' betting, and they were waiting anxiously for the Swordbearer to emerge among those betting to remove the sword from the rock.

The Knights were so caught up in their gambling frenzy that they didn't hear the ringing of Camelot's emergence bell. This showed just how perfect Prince Arthur's plan was to sneak his way to the sword buried in the rock without any guards noticing or preventing him.

When the man in a prince's armor vest finally made it to 'The Kings' Sword's' resting place, the voice calling out to him grew louder and louder. A man approached the man in a prince's armor and told him to line up with the others, waiting for their turn to try pulling the sword out of the rock.

The man in a prince's armor suit was the seventh man on the line. More than 254,352 volunteers from all over the world had participated but failed to pull 'The Kings' Sword' out of the rock. The sword-pulling contest kicked off every day and ran late into the evening, with more and more people flocking from different Kingdoms to watch the competition organized by gamblers. By the seventh month of the contest, 'The Kings' Sword' pulling challenge was still going strong, and it kept gamblers hooked since everyone believed it was finally time for the sword to leave the rock.

The gamblers placed a twenty-thousand gold coin bet on the first guy in front of the man in the prince's armor who stepped up to try pulling 'The Kings' Sword' from the rock. The gamblers used a sandglass watch as a timer for every participant or volunteer to make it a fair game.

As the time of the first man ended because he failed to pull 'The Kings' Sword' out of the rock, it became the turn of the second volunteer. The second volunteer wanting to 'The Kings' Sword' out of the rock was a short but muscular person. He removes his clothes to expose his muscular chest to the cheering ladies that he was capable of pulling 'The Kings' Sword' from the rock. The betting prince increased to forty thousand gold coins. The second man (the most muscular person to ever emerge as a participant), trying his luck to pull 'The Kings' Sword' out of the rock, also failed just like the first man.

The atmosphere at 'The Kings' Sword competition changed immediately as the third man stepped forward. This is because the third competitor was a huge man which made him gain more cheering and clapping for the entertaining audience. As a result, the gamblers bet eighty thousand gold coins for him if he is successful in pulling 'The Kings' Sword' out of the rock. Then, the third man shows his appreciation to the gamblers and his fans among the crowd by showing them his powerful hand and muscles. Consequently, he receives more cheers than the last competitor. He puts his muscular hands on the 'The Kings' Sword' but struggles in vain to pull the sword from the rock. As a result, the third person failed because his time ended, and he was unable to pull 'The

Kings' Sword' from the rock. He walks away disappointedly because he has let down his cheering crowd and fans wanting to see a muscular person lift 'The Kings' Sword' from the rock.

Interestingly, the resting place of 'The Kings' Sword' became more populated as different people who weren't gamblers paid heavily to watch the volunteers try their luck whether they could pull 'The Kings' Sword' out of the rock. All the inns in Camelot were filled up because there were many people who came to witness the pulling of 'The Kings' Sword' out of the rock. People slept outside to rent out their homes to 'The Kings' Sword' visitors visiting the resting place of the sword's site because they were paid a good sum of money for the rent their homes provided. Market women and men enjoyed good sales because there were plenty of things to sell to the ever-growing visitors visiting and watching 'The Kings' Sword' pulling from the rock competition.

The Queen's officials receive tremendous amounts of taxes from visitors, gamblers, and market sellers. These were some things that had never happened before in Camelot. Indeed, 'The Kings' Sword' brought riches and prosperity to everyone in Camelot even before it left its resting place to fulfill the prophecy of wealth for the people.

The fourth man stepped out. He was a hairy man who frightened most people with his terrible looks. This made people fear while others laughed and enjoyed themselves, viewing the event as it unfolded. The announcer hyped up the hairy man, saying he'd win a whopping 150,000 gold coins if he could pull 'The Kings' Sword' out of the rock. Just like his previous contestants before him, the hairy man, who was the fourth contestant, totally failed. He gave up and stormed off after his first attempt, proving he didn't stand a chance of pulling 'The Kings' Sword' out of the rock.

It was the time for the fifth person to try his luck to determine whether he also could pull 'The Kings' Sword' out of the rock. The fifth person was the tallest man who had entered into the sword-pulling contest. He raised his hands up and clapped and, as a result, received more cheers from the cheering crowd. He was promised four hundred thousand gold coins if he could pull 'The Kings' Sword' out of the rock. The ladies' presence gave him lovely smiles. This meant the tall man might score a shot at marrying one of the gorgeous ladies if he actually managed to succeed. Sadly, he was unsuccessful because he failed to pull 'The Kings' Sword' out of the rock like others. He even got angry with the man who rang a bell, signifying that his time was over.

The resting place of 'The Kings' Sword' became more exciting and enjoyable as the crowd (people watching) started laughing and jubilating whenever a contestant that they didn't support failed.

Right then, the soldiers from the castle came to the scene searching for the man in a prince's armor suit with some Knights. Gaius also followed the soldiers because they suspected that the man in a prince's armor suit headed toward the resting place of the sword.

The sixth person just walked away after seeing most people fail who he thought could pull 'The Kings' Sword' out of the rock. An announcer announces to the enthusiastic crowd, "Five hundred thousand gold coins for any man who could pull 'The Kings' Sword' out of the rock."

Then, the man in a prince's armor stepped forward, but surprisingly, nobody cheered. This is because he was the smallest person ever seen as a contestant since the beginning of the tournament. Some people in the crowd started bullying him, while others began to throw small things at him. Some even started calling him funny names, which made the scene more exciting. Some secret knights who had been sent by the Queen earlier were present at the scene, starting to laugh at his poorly dressed Prince's armed suit. The soldiers and their Knights started surrounding the place to arrest him for kidnapping Prince Arthur.

Suddenly, a flash of sunlight appeared on the man in the prince's armor. He put his right hand on the sword's handle (hilt). Then, the grounds started shaking, and there came strong winds. Also, there was an earthquake that shook the Queen's castle. Queen Gwen could see the man in a prince's armor from her window. Queen Gwen also joined in viewing what would eventually happen. She even asks herself if the man in a prince's suit could be the rightful sword wielder. The crowd became afraid because such a thing had never happened since the beginning of the sword-pulling contest. Then, the ground shaking and the wind blowing suddenly stopped. The sword's brightness became brighter, and colorful birds surrounded the man in a prince's armor. The man in a prince's armor started pulling 'The Kings' Sword' out of the rock easily. People became silent because they could see him pulling 'The Kings' Sword' out of the rock until he pulled it out successfully. He raises The Kings' Sword' towards the sky where lightens connects to the sword. Then, he pointed 'The Kings' Sword' to the crowd, and everyone started to kneel as a sign of respect for the King. Even the

Knights also did the same thing, except Sir Leon. Queen Gwen wondered who such a man could be.

A picture of Prince Arthur removing 'The Kings' Sword from the rock.

Sir Leon ordered the soldiers to arrest the man in the prince's armor. Sir Leon told him to take off his helmet so that they could see his face. The man in the prince's armor took off his helmet, and bam—it was Prince Arthur. Just then, Emrys (Merlin) showed up at the place and told everyone to kneel for Prince Arthur. Emrys announces, "From today onwards, Prince Arthur Pendragon is now the rightful bearer of The Kings' Sword." This time, Sir Leon and his Knights and the whole crowd knelt again for Prince Arthur as Emrys grabbed Arthur's left hand and led him to the Queen's castle. Sir Leon grabbed the box with the five hundred thousand gold coins and followed Emrys and Prince Arthur to the Queen's palace.

CHAPTER FOUR

THE WONDERS OF PRINCE ARTHUR'S SWORD AS 'THE KINGS' SWORD' BEARER

Emrys, Prince Arthur, the Knights, and the soldiers came to meet Queen Gwen. Queen Gwen was speechless for some time because she couldn't believe how a young lad managed to outsmart her intelligent guards. Gaius figured that the Queen was still confused about today's events and hadn't said a word yet. Gaius decides to approach the Queen to make her say something. Gaius leaned over and whispered to the Queen, saying, "Let's welcome our Swordbearer first, then we will decide on what to do next." Queen said, "It's surprising that the wielder of 'The King's Sword' we've been waiting for turned out to be Prince Arthur. We will celebrate today as an important day with 'The Kings' Sword' finally returning to the Pendragon family. Henceforth, Prince Arthur would have a seat in the Royal Council Meeting. The castle treasurer would keep the five hundred thousand gold coins for future use. Thanks, everyone."

Queen Gwen continues, "Everyone could now take

their leave except the Royal Council Members who should stay behind for an important meeting." Queen Gwen told Emrys, "Please, join us in the meeting." Queen Gwen sat on her throne, and Prince Arthur sat on his Prince's seat (next to the Queen), and all the Knights, including Merlin and Gaius, also took their seats as Members of the Royal Council.

Queen Gwen says, "Because of todays' event, everyone around the world, now know that Camelot possesses the 'The Kings' Sword' which has some good and bad benefits. My greatest fear is that other Kingdoms might start waging war against Camelot in order to get their hand on the sword. Some desperate and wicked ones who doesn't support Albion's prosperities might send assassins to eliminate the Prince who is now the Sword wielder. Many people would continue to visit Camelot from around the world just to see the Prince with 'The Kings' Sword' in his hand. These are problems confronting this Kingdom now. Therefore, starting from tomorrow, the preparations for war would start, we must be prepared for war if any Kingdom would launch a surprise attacked on Camelot because of 'The Kings' Sword' in our possession."

Queen Gwen called on Sir Leon, and he stood up as a sign of respect for the Queen. "You would be in charge of the war preparations. You're free to recruit more men to boost Camelot's security. We mustn't let our guard down. We would use the bet money won by Prince Arthur to finance our war preparations. We must be prepared for any eventualities, as far as 'The Kings' Sword' is concerned." Said Queen Gwen. "As For you (Emrys), you will be in charge of mentoring Prince Arthur. Prince Arthur still has a lot to learn regarding the sword." Said Queen Gwen.

The meeting got cut off when Galador barged into the Royal Council room. Galador shouted, "Pardon me for coming late, my Queen!" Right away, everyone at the meeting stood up because they knew the prophecy, making Galador live up to 500 years without dying. Galador shouted again, "My Prince, so it's true, you're 'The Kings' Sword' bearer?" Galador continues, "Please, bless my soul so that I can rest in peace." Everybody in the Royal Council meeting stood up, waiting to see what would eventually happen to Galador after the prophecy had come through that he wouldn't die until he saw 'The Kings' Sword wielder with his own eyes.

Prince Arthur got to his feet and said, "I'm sorry for the pain my household has caused you. I set your soul free. You're blessed by 'The Kings' Swordbearer." Prince Arthur places 'The Kings'

Sword on Galador's body.

In the presence of Merlin, Gaius, Queen Gwen, and all the Knights of Camelot (dressed in traditional reddish clothes), Prince Arthur blessing Galador with 'The Kings' Sword' as the Swordbearer in the castle.

Suddenly, Galador collapses to the ground and dies. He had lived for over 500 years without dying because he had to see the sword bearer before he died.

Queen Gwen became speechless because nobody taught Prince Arthur how to use the sword. The royal guards picked up Galador's lifeless body and carried him away. Queen Gwen gave orders for Galador to be buried like a King. The Royal Council Members couldn't settle down to their seats, and the meeting ended as the Queen left with Prince Arthur.

More people believed in the powers of 'The King's Sword' in Camelot, and the news spread far to other Kingdoms like a wide burning fire. The Kings' Sword news finally got to one of Albion's sworn enemies, who happens to be King Vortigern. His spies brought him the news about Prince Arthur pulling 'The Kings' Sword' from the rock.

King Vortigern's mother, Queen Viviane, was burned at the stake along with a witch by the late King Uther Pendragon. King Vortigern hadn't attended his throne by that time to avenge his mother's disgraceful death on the burning stick. King Vortigern swore that he would have his revenge on the late King Uther himself or King Uther's children, even grandchildren, as long as he was still alive. King Vortigern sent for the most dangerous assassin.

Caradoc is the most dangerous assassin trained by the sea pirates. He is the only deadliest killer who has successfully penetrated deep into a king's heavily guarded palace to accomplish his killing assignment. The fact that Caradoc killed the Saxon's King and 40 of his strongest guards inside a royal palace terrified everyone. One of Caradoc's killing strategies is that people don't recognize him as somebody capable of killing because he is the shortest assassin.

Also, Caradoc was fast in attacking his victims. Using various killing weapons and skills, he could kill over 50 bravest guards within a minute. To add to his killing capabilities, Caradoc's skin, especially his chest, is impenetrable to any arrow or blade entering. Therefore, Caradoc can't be assassinated or killed by an arrow or ordinary sword made by any human. All these made Caradoc the devil's soul-hunting tools that man has ever seen.

Caradoc arrives at King Vortigern's heavily guarded palace in case he decides to assassinate the King himself instead of Prince Arthur. King Vortigern said, "I want you to kill Prince Arthur Pendragon because his grandfather (late Uther Pendragon) took away my mother (Queen

Viviane), who was dared to me. He didn't respect the royal bond among Kings from other Kingdoms. Queen Viviane was visiting a powerful witch (Hecate) in Camelot to get my healing medicine when she was arrested by Uther's men. Uther burnt Queen Viviane, who was our Queen in this Kingdom, to a stick together with a witch (Hecate) who the Queen was visiting."

King Vortigern continues after tears fall from his eyes as he talks to Caradoc, "My mother (Our late Queen Viviane) was my hero because she saved the life of one of her secret guards so he could escape with the medicine in order to get me well. Therefore, I owed our Queen Viviane a debt to kill one of Camelot's royal bloods as an act of revenge for my mother's disgraceful death. I need to kill someone who is very daring to Camelot's throne. The death of an important Pendragon family member would satisfy my hungry urge for revenge."

King Vortigern's guards pulled out their swords when they saw Caradoc holding their King's hands. They were ready to attack Caradoc if he dared hurt or kill their King. Caradoc sympathizes with King Vortigern by saying, "I know that holding the King's hands is an offense in your Kingdom for an ordinary person isn't permitted to hold a royal person, but I did this to sympathize with you that Prince Arthur Pendragon would be dead by the time I get to Camelot in three weeks." "Then I'll reward you heavily upon your return if you're successful. Take a five thousand gold coins as your expenses for this mission. Good luck. You may take your leave." Said King Vortigern. Caradoc left King Vortigern's palace and headed on his journey towards Camelot.

Back in Camelot, Prince Arthur and Queen Gwen were having breakfast at the royal dining table. Queen Gwen has been watching Prince Arthur for some time. She wonders how Prince Arthur is mastering his royal duties successfully since he pulled 'The Kings' Sword from the rock without much supervision. Prince Arthur said to Queen Gwen, "Mother, I feel uneased because of the way you're looking at me."

Queen Gwen responded, "I'm sorry, my son. It's just because you surprise me most of the time. For instance, you broke into your late dad's closet and took his princely armor that your father worn when he was young. You even went ahead and put on his princely uniform; even though it didn't fit you. You never thought of returning your dad's princely suit. You wore it every day as if you were going to war."

Prince Arthur responds, "I'm sorry, mother." "I'm a Queen and also a caring mother, but you sometimes make decisions without consulting me. There are times you would go into hiding just because you wanted to be with your friends (Merlin, Gaius, and Emrys)." Said Queen Gwen. Queen Gwen continues, "The worst one is when you put on your late dad's prince uniform and went to 'The Kings' Sword' resting place without telling your mother."

Prince Arthur said, "I'm sorry, My Queen. It wouldn't happen again." Queen replied warmly, "Apologies, accepted."

Suddenly, Emrys arrives at the Queen's dining table with Gaius. "I've brought your medicine, my Queen. The medicine will help you to eat and sleep well." Said Gaius. Emrys says, "Prince Arthur and I are going to the training ground." Queen asks Prince Arthur, "You didn't mention that to me this morning. Well, you've promised never to hide anything from your mother."

Prince Arthur said, "I've told Emrys yesterday that I would join the training. I wanted to learn how to be a skillful Knight so that I can protect you, mother."

Queen Gwen said, "That is the loveliest word you've ever said to me since you were born." Prince Arthur asks Queen Gwen, "Do I have your permission to go to the Knights' training ground?"

"Yes! Yes! It's your royal duties to protect your Queen but you must be careful because you still have a lot to learn from Sir Leon who is your trainer." Prince Arthur jumped up from his chair and gave his mother a hug (Queen Gwen).

Prince Arthur and Emrys left for the training ground. Queen Gwen said to Gaius, "Sometimes I wonder why Prince Arthur behaves so much like his late father (King Arthur Pendragon)." Gaius and Queen Gwen smile at Prince Arthur and Emrys going to the training ground. Gaius said within himself, "In fact, he's truly your dead husband."

Sir Leon was on the training ground as ordered by Queen Gwen. Sir Leon had assembled newly recruited Knights and soldiers for training. The Knights and soldiers assembled separately, ready to take training orders from Sir Leon. Whenever Sir Leon gives orders, the mounted Knights on horses, Knights, and soldiers on foot carry out the orders as instructed in a coordinated and orderly manner.

When Sir Leon says, "attack to your right." Knights and soldiers responded by saying, "Aye, Sir!" As the Knights (both on horses and on foot), including foot soldiers, quickly turn their heads, followed by a pivot of their bodies facing their right side. They shift accordingly, maintaining their formation to ensure optimal striking positions. Mounted Knights, foot Knights, and soldiers gripped their weapons firmly, ready for action.

On the other hand, when Sir Leon says, "Attack to your left." The Knights and soldiers acknowledge Sir Leon by saying, "Yes, Sir!" As the Knights (both on horses and on foot), including foot soldiers, quickly turn their attention to the left. Foot soldiers with their spears lunge onwards in the left direction, and Knights with their swords step forward towards the left. At the same time, mounted Knights direct their horses to charge to the left in readiness to strike. Militarily, the men ensured they had enough space to wield their weapons effectively, regardless of whether they were ordered to the left or right.

Sir Percival, who was the squad leader on the training ground, said, "Here comes 'The Kings' Swordbearer to the training ground."

Sir Leon said, "Welcome, my Prince. I hope you want to watch today's training session?" "No, I'm here to join the training session." Said Prince Arthur. Sir Leon looked at Sir Percival and Emrys before replying to Prince Arthur, saying, "We have gone far into the training process. I'm afraid you can't catch up with my trainees because they have learnt a lot of combat skills but you didn't have any."

Prince Arthur said to Sir Leon, "Choose seven of your best combat students for a competition. If they beat me, I wouldn't join your training lessons but if I beat them, then I will join your training class. Don't worry, Sir Leon, I won't hurt them neither they won't hurt me."

Sir Percival rang the training bell, which signifies the beginning of a combat competition among the training Knights. Sir Leon went to meet Sir Percival beside the training bell and whispered into his ear, Sir Percival, why do you ring the bell? You know Prince Arthur has no combat skills yet. He might get hurt, and we will all be in big trouble with the Queen. "Don't worry, let us trust Prince Arthur's words. He sounds like the late King Arthur Pendragon. Besides, we would be helpless if Prince Arthur get us orders that he wants to join the training session." Replied Sir Percival.

Unknowingly, to Sir Percival and Sir Leon, Queen Gwen and Gaius were watching from the window. Queen Gwen told Gaius, "I would have to stop this fight. The Prince shouldn't be allowed to be drawn into a combat fight when he hasn't gotten any combative skills." Gaius said to Queen Gwen, "Let us wait and see what happens before stopping the fight."

Seven Knights surrounded Prince Arthur. The first Knight (Sir Gareth) said let me try our newcomer. The other Knights laugh at Prince Arthur, expecting Sir Gareth to beat Prince Arthur so easily. Sir Gareth charged and came running towards Prince Arthur in a slow motion. Prince Arthur's sword shone as he aimed at Sir Gareth's legs. Prince Arthur bent down and raised Sir Gareth high into the sky. Sir Gareth fell down helpless with his face covered with mud. Also, his sword fell off from his hand. Prince Arthur stood on the back of the first Knight. He then places his sword on Sir Gareth's neck. This signifies that Sir Gareth has lost the competition. Sir Percival laughed and pulled the first Knight (Sir Gareth) out of the competition.

The second Knight (Sir Tristan) was tall and muscular in size. He waves his sword to show Prince Arthur that he knows how to use the sword better than the first Knight (Sir Gareth). Sir Tristan runs towards Prince Arthur, who is displaying his sword. Prince Arthur's sword shone, and he also charged toward Sir Tristan. Prince Arthur jumps high into the sky and over Sir Tristan's head. Prince Arthur hits Sir Tristan on the back of his head while he is still in the sky. Sir Tristan fell disgracefully to the ground with his face also covered with mud, and his sword fell off his hand. Prince Arthur landed on Sir Tristan's back. He places his sword on the back of Sir Tristan's neck. All these actions happened in a slow motion.

Sir Percival laughs again and claps his hands for Prince Arthur before pulling the second Knight (Sir Tristan) out of the competition.

The news of Prince Arthur's victories in the training attracted many of his fans who watched him pull 'The King Sword' from the rock. Soon, the population at the training ground was more than that of 'The Kings' Sword' pulling competition.

Unknown to many people present at the training ground, Morgana Pendragon was on the training ground. She got to 'The Kings' Sword' pulling competition late, but she was fortunate to watch Prince Arthur in action. She covered her head and most of her body with a black cloth so that no one would recognize her. Morgana Pendragon wanted to know the secrets of 'The King Sword.'

The third Knight (Sir Lamorak) gave a sign to the fourth Knight (Sir Ector), indicating that both of them should fight Prince Arthur together. Sir Lamorak and Sir Ector put on their helmets and surrounded Prince Arthur. Prince Arthur's sword shines for the third time. The two Knights charged at the same time towards Prince Arthur. Sir Lamorak was coming in front of Prince Arthur while Sir Ector was attacking Prince Arthur from behind. Thus, Prince Arthur was in the middle of the two Knights. Prince Arthur quickly bent down, and both Knights clashed their helmets against themselves (in a slow motion). Prince Arthur knocked out both Knights with his fists. They fell and couldn't get up. This made everyone laugh. This was when Sir Percival and Sir Leon knew that Queen and Gaius were laughing from the castle's window upsteps.

Prince Arthur's triumphs at the training ground made the remaining three Knights (Sir Dagonet, Sir Pelleas, and Sir Brunor) withdraw their attacks because skillful mounted Knights had shown their interest in attacking Prince Arthur on horses from different directions.

Sir Leodegrance, Sir Galahad, and Sir Agravain, who were the most skillful, charge their horses towards Prince Arthur. Sir Percival rings the bell for the second time to signify the beginning of another phase of the competition by shouting, "I love today's tournament more than the pulling of 'The Kings' Sword' from the rock."

Sir Leodegrance, Sir Galahad, and Sir Agravain's horses face Prince Arthur, who is just holding a sword in his hand and isn't on a horse like his competitors. Prince Arthur's sword (The Kings' Sword) shines as usual whenever there is a potential fight against the Swordbearer. In a slow motion, the three Knights charged their horses toward Prince Arthur, who was facing Sir Galahad's horse in the middle. Prince Arthur could hear the voices of cheering crowds because everyone liked him since he successfully pulled 'The Kings' Sword from the rock. Unlike the other time when he was bullied by the crowd that never expected him to win. Prince Arthur held his middle position.

Queen Gwen started getting worried. Queen Gwen shouted to Prince Arthur, saying, "Don't just stand there like a tree, my son, attack them or you will get hurt." Unfortunately, Prince Arthur can't hear her. She closed her eyes and covered her face with her hands because Queen Gwen was too afraid to watch. In a slow motion, just as the three Knights almost strike Prince Arthur, he moves swiftly to the left and hits the left leg of Sir Leodegrance's horse. Sir Leodegrance's horse lifted him high into the sky, and both Sir Leodegrance and his horse somersaulted thrice on the muddy training ground. This made the whole crowd to start jubilating, and joy filled the air.

The crowd started yelling: 'Prince Arthur! Prince Arthur!! Prince Arthur!!! The cheering crowd's voices made Queen Gwen open her eyes because she could hear that her son (Prince Arthur) was winning. Queen also joined in cheering Prince Arthur even when she didn't know how he won Sir Leodegrance. Queen Gwen's loud cheering at her window attracted her maids, who also watched the tournament.

The remaining two Knights, Sir Galahad and Sir Agravain moved close and started discussing. Sir Leon moves closer to Sir Percival, saying, "This is crazy! You've to stop this match. As the squad leader, you know that they would eventually strategize their war plan whenever they stopped fighting and started discussing among themselves. This is because we taught them to do so. They might hurt the Prince when the Knights reorganize their tactics. We shouldn't let the Prince get hurt." Sir Percival holds Sir Leon's hands and says, "My friend, see the whole of Camelot are here even Queen Gwen is watching from up steps. If Prince Arthur wins, the people would be happy because they will feel secure that our late King is back. Don't worry, I will take responsibility for whatever happens here today."

Just then, Sir Galahad and Sir Agravain completed the strategizing on what tactics to use in order to defeat Prince Arthur. They gave Sir Percival a sign to ring the bell. There was complete silence among the crowd at the tournament venue, who were eagerly waiting to see what would happen. Prince Arthur's sword shines as usual.

Morgana Pendragon now discovered the secrets helping Prince Arthur to win. Morgana Pendragon says within her mind, "So my stepbrother uses 'The Kings' Sword' to win his fights. I'll make him fail and even kill him right here in front of his people."

Unlike before, Sir Galahad and Sir Agravain didn't charge toward Prince Arthur. The two Knights encircle Prince Arthur. They aimed to form a narrow encirclement around Prince Arthur, which would eventually give them a good striking position since other tactics had failed. So, each Knight takes their time moving around Prince Arthur on a horse. As a result, their encirclement becomes narrower and deadlier for Prince Arthur to defend himself effectively. This would give them the opportunity to strike the Prince easily.

Prince Arthur quickly landed on Sir Galahad's horse's back, hitting Sir Galahad's helmet with his sword's hilt (sword handle). Sir Galahad fainted and fell off his horse.

The silence covering the crowd stopped, and once again, the whole crowd started cheering again for Prince Arthur. Sir Agravain now becomes the last man standing against Prince Arthur. Prince

Arthur now raised his sword to appreciate the whole crowd. Queen Gwen shouted, "Get down from the horse, my son. Sir Agrawain is a more experienced horseman than you. But Prince Arthur couldn't hear the Queen because of the loud cheers from the crowd." Sir Agravain became afraid because he had underrated Prince Arthur as an inexperienced swordsperson.

Prince Arthur became carried away by the crowd's jubilant cheers for him. As a result, he doesn't listen to the voice coming from 'The Kings' Sword' that he is wielding. The sword was the magic talking and directing Prince Arthur that enabled him to go so far into this tournament. Prince Arthur charged his horse towards Sir Agravain. This is because Prince Arthur sighted that Sir Agravain was too afraid to attack even when the voice from his sword (The Kings' Sword) didn't tell him to do so.

Morgana Pendragon quickly knows it is time to carry out her evil plan. She observes that Prince Arthur didn't wait for the sword to shine before he charged towards Sir Agravain.

Morgana Pendragon's eyes turned red as she eyed the leather holding Prince Arthur's horse stirrup. As a result, Prince Arthur fell from his horse, rolling on the muddy ground continuously. Morgana Pendragon smiles. She also eyed Sir

Agravain and controlled him by saying, "Go and kill him, you fool."

Emrys suspected something was wrong. He started viewing the crowd because he had no other person in his mind apart from Morgana Pendragon. Emrys suspects someone with wicked magic, like Morgana Pendragon, to be among the crowd. Emrys also heard that Sir Agravain was commanded to kill Prince Arthur.

In a slow motion, Sir Leon started running towards the bell in order to end the match to save Prince Arthur's life.

Prince Arthur defeating seven Knights in a contest on the training ground.

Also, in slow motion, Sir Agravain, who was now under Morgana's control, reared his horse high and charged his horse toward Prince Arthur, who was still rolling in the mud. Queen Gwen fainted, and her maids started pouring water on her head to revive her. As Prince Arthur was still rolling on the muddy ground, there came the voice from the sword saying, "Always listen to me, young Prince

Arthur, if you want to live." Prince Arthur's response in his mind was, "I'm sorry." The voice from the sword continued, saying, "Continue to roll until I ask you to stop. Then, you will bend down and hit his horse with your sword's hilt. Just get ready."

As Sir Agravain was about to strike Prince Arthur with his sword, Prince Arthur moved swiftly under Sir Agravain's horse. He hit the underneath of the horse harder with his sword's hits. As a result, Sir Agravain loses balance while on top speed. This made Sir Agravain fall harder on the muddy ground, and he fainted with his body covered with mud while his horse remained unconscious on the mud as well.

That was when Sir Leon reached the bell, and he rang it, signifying the end of the tournament. The crowd broke down the foot soldiers' barriers, preventing them from entering the training ground to lift up their hero, Prince Arthur Pendragon. The crowd started jubilating. The crowd's jubilations were so loud that it revived Queen Gwen, who once missed the action the second time.

The only person who remained still without jubilating was a lady covered in dark clothes. Emrys approached the lady and said, "You ought to have known by now, Morgana, that you'll never kill Arthur Pendragon. He's now reborn to remain alive." Morgana Pendragon removed the dark clothes covering her face and said, "I'll be back again."

Queen Gwen and Gaius could see and recognize Morgana Pendragon from the castle window when Emrys was talking to her. Morgana Pendragon disappeared, but no one knew Morgana Pendragon was at the tournament except Gaius, Emrys, and Queen Gwen.

CHAPTER FIVE

PRINCE ARTHUR'S DEADLY ENCOUNTER WITH THE FEARLESS ASSASSIN

There were continuous jubilations not only in Camelot but throughout Albion as a whole. The people viewed Prince Arthur as King Arthur himself without any differences because of his heroic deeds. Queen Gwen, Gaius, including some Knights (who weren't at the training ground but got the news) came to the training ground to congratulate Prince Arthur. Queen Gwen said, "I would allow Sir Leon to make his pronouncement. He surely has something to say concerning the Prince."

Sir Leon stood forward, facing the crowd who had witnessed the fight, saying, "Today, our Prince has proven to be a hero. Prince Arthur won all the challenges to become qualified to become a professional trainee. As a result, he is now a member of our elite Knights. Prince Arthur is just a trainee Knight, who earned the title of a leader to command other Knights into battle whenever needed. Even though Prince Arthur has become the youngest professional Knight that Camelot has ever produced. Starting from today onwards, Prince Arthur will begin to train other Knights. His father (the late King Arthur Pendragon) held this position before he died. Thank you for the cheers and jubilations given to our Prince."

Queen Gwen, Gaius, and other entourages left for the castle. The cheering crowd also disappeared. Only Emrys and Prince were left on the training ground. Prince Arthur sat down, looking worried. Emrys noticed the unhappiness on the Prince's face. Emrys asks Prince Arthur, "Is anything wrong? You look so unhappy." "Yes, something tells me that Queen is unhappy that I risked my life to prove myself worthy as a skillful Knight." Replied Prince Arthur. "Don't worry. We'll think of a way to make your mother see the reasons why you need to train. But you need to clean up first." Said Emrys.

Prince Arthur and Emrys had just left for the castle when Caradoc got to Camelot. His first task is to rent a room which faces the castle's entrance. This would enable Caradoc to monitor Prince Arthur's movements so that he could assassinate him easily.

Caradoc bought apples from an apple seller in the market. He asks the apple seller, "They say the Queen's place isn't far from here?" "Yes, it's over there. It seems you just got to Camelot. Then you have missed the contests. Firstly, the mountain over there was the former resting place of the great Kings' Sword. Our bravest Prince is now the Swordbearer. Prince Arthur got great fighting skills because he single-handedly defeated Knights on horses and foot." Said the apple seller.

Caradoc was able to locate the Queen's palace through his discussions with the apple seller from the market. Caradoc said to himself, "I need to get a good shooting range to the palace from any inn window." He finally got an inn whose window faces the entrance of the Queen's palace. Caradoc checked into the inn, but he was met with an unfriendly welcome by the man in charge of the inn. "There wasn't any space for you at this moment; please check another inn nearby." Said the man in charge of the inn as he was sweeping the floor. Caradoc said, "100 gold coins for the room whose window faces the Queen's palace." I'm not interested because it's my personal room. Take your money elsewhere." Replied the man in charge of the inn. "Then I will pay 500 gold coins for your room." Said Caradoc as he negotiated with the man at the inn. "500 gold coins for the room per day." Replied the man at the inn. "Deal!" Agreed, said Caradoc. "I will sleep in the bar for the first time." Said the man at the inn.

Caradoc rented the room facing the palace

entrance. Caradoc could see everyone going in and out of the palace. The first person Caradoc saw was a young man coming out of the palace's gates. Caradoc saw that children surrounded the young man and they were waving Albion's flags. Caradoc said to himself, "This must be Prince Arthur." He took a small crossbow with an arrow. Caradoc aims at the young man he thought could be the Prince. The children don't give him enough space for Caradoc to aim at his target.

Caradoc finally took a reckless shot, which struck one of the children. Merlin quickly carried the child into the palace to meet Gaius. Gaius asked Merlin what had happened. Merlin explained that the arrow was meant for him but had accidentally struck the child. Gaius told Merlin that he needed to use his magic powers to heal the child because the child was losing much blood and might die at any time. Gaius closed the door so that Merlin could heal the child with his magical powers.

Caradoc saw from his inn window that many Knights and other royal guests were present for an important ceremony. Many dignities gathered in Camelot's second hall because it was the Knights' induction ceremony. Interestingly, it was also Prince Arthur's Knight's induction ceremony. Queen Gwen had put Arthur's assassination attempt behind her. Queen Gwen was happy that she was the mother of the bravest Knight, who was also the Swordbearer. The older Knights stood behind Queen Gwen while the newly inducted Knights stood in her front, knelt before her, waiting for the Queen's blessings.

As a result, the whole hall was adorned with reddish Knights uniforms. The Knights recite their royal pledge, saying:

"As a royal Knight, I solemnly pledge to uphold honor and justice in all my actions. To defend the weak and protect the innocent. To serve my Kingdom and my fellow Knights with loyalty and courage. To maintain the virtues of truth, humility, and chivalry. To strive for excellence and wisdom in all my endeavors. To be loyal to my King or Queen. I will remain be faithful to my vows and my duty, always and forever."

Queen placed her sword on Sir Bedivere, saying, "Rise, Sir Bedivere, Knight of Camelot." Queen Gwen also placed her sword on Sir Galahad's head, saying, "Rise, Sir Galahad...Knight of Camelot." Queen Gwen placed her sword on Knight's head, saying, "Rise, Sir Tristan......Knight of Camelot." Queen Gwen moved to another Knight kneeling, saying, "Rise, Sir Gareth......Knight of Camelot." Queen Gwen steps to another waiting Kneeling, saying, "Rise, Sir

Agravain………Knight of Camelot." Queen Gwen says to the next waiting Knight, "Rise, Sir Palamedes…………Knight of Camelot." Queen Gwen goes to another Knight who is kneeling, saying, "Rise, Sir Ector………Knight of Camelot." Queen Gwen went to another Knight kneeling, saying, "Rise, Sir Lamorak………Knight of Camelot." Queen Gwen turns to another Knight still kneeling, saying, "Rise Sir Gaheris………Knight of Camelot." Queen Gwen goes to another Knight kneeling, saying, "Rise Sir Dagonet……Knight of Camelot." Queen Gwen places her sword on another Knight, saying, "Rise Sir Uwaine………Knight of Camelot." Queen Gwen goes to another Knight kneeling, placing her sword on his head, saying, "Rise Sir Safir……Knight of Camelot." Queen Gwen turns her sword to the head of another Knight who was kneeling, saying, "Rise Sir Tor………Knight of Camelot." Queen Gwen moves her sword to another Knight's head who was kneeling, saying, "Rise Sir Alymere……. Knight of Camelot." Queen Gwen goes to another who is kneeling, saying, "Rise Sir Brunor………Knight of Camelot." Queen Gwen places her sword on another Knight's head who was kneeling, saying, "Rise Sir Leodegrance……Knight of Camelot." Queen Gwen goes to where another Knight who is kneeling, saying, "Rise Sir Pelleas………Knight of Camelot."

Queen Gwen goes where another was kneeling, saying, "Rise Sir Marrok.......... Knight of Camelot." Queen Gwen went to the place where another Knight was kneeling down, saying, "Rise Sir Amren.........Knight of Camelot." Queen Gwen places her sword on another Knight's head, saying, "Rise Sir Morholt..........Knight of Camelot." Queen Gwen goes to where another Knight who is kneeling, and she places her sword on his head, saying, "Rise Sir Sagremor.........Knight of Camelot." Queen Gwen goes to where Sir Baudwin is kneeling, and she places her sword on Sir Baudwin's head, saying, "Rise Sir Baudwin.........Knight of Camelot." Queen Gwen moves to where Sir Elyan is kneeling, and Queen Gwen places her sword on Sir Elyan's head, saying, "Rise Sir Elyan......Knight of Camelot." Queen Gwen goes to where Sir Mador is kneeling, and she places her sword on Sir Mador's head, saying, "Rise Sir Mador.........Knight of Camelot."

Then, Camelot's trumpets sounded, signaling that it was Prince Arthur's turn to be inducted by Queen Gwen. This was the perfect time that Caradoc had been waiting for to shoot at Prince Arthur far from his room. He had waited patiently for the ideal shooting time to kill Prince Arthur with his long-range weapon. Caradoc placed his short crossbow and arrow in position. Queen

Gwen and her Knights, including old and newly inducted Knights, surrounded Prince Arthur. Caradoc could see Prince Arthur clearly from among other Knights, which was a rare opportunity for him to shot.

There came a knock on Caradoc's door, which distracted his aim, and his arrow struck Sir Gaheris' shoulder, revealing that an assassin was targeting the Prince for the second time. The royal guards quickly surround the Queen and Prince Arthur while Gaius attends to Sir Gaheris' wound. Caradoc opens his door to find a lady carrying the food that he ordered. He paid for his food, and the lady left. No one in the inn suspects that Caradoc is an assassin.

The soldiers at the palace entrance were on high alert because they knew that there was an assassin in town who wanted Prince Arthur dead. The news of the assassin's mistakes got to Queen and Prince Arthur. Queen summons Sir Leon and Sir Percival, who are Camelot's most experienced swordsmen.

Sir Percival told Queen Gwen, "The killer was nearly by the castle because he used a shorter and deadlier arrow. The assassin is capable of aiming at anybody with his weapon because he has a good shooting range. We will check all the houses close to the palace's entrance." Sir Leon and Sir Percival left the Queen to begin their search for the assassin.

Queen Gwen asks Gaius about the child's condition. Gaius says, "The child's condition is stable now. He will be with family tonight after taking his medicine." Queen Gwen said, "That is good news. Let's pray that Sir Leon and Sir Percival catch up with the killer on time before he mistakenly kills another innocent person, thinking he is the Prince."

The assassin came down steps to hear if the people drinking were discussing about the assassination attempt on the Prince's life. Nobody among the people drinking at the bar mentioned that soldiers were trailing the assassin.

At midnight, the assassin climbs to the palace wall like a spider as he searches each palace window for the Prince. Prince Arthur's sword began to shine, which drew Arthur's attention. Arthur holds the sword, and he notices the assassin on the castle's wall. The assassin was listening to the discussion of some Knights, Gaius, Merlin, and Queen Gwen. The assassin says to himself, "I'll kill Camelot's Queen since it's difficult finding and killing the Prince. The price for killing the Queen would be huge." The killer aimed his weapon at Queen Gwen from the castle's wall he was hanging on.

In slow motion, Prince Arthur ran and broke into the room where Queen Gwen, through the Knights, Merlin, and Gaius were. Prince Arthur threw 'The King's Sword,' which passed close to Queen Gwen's head, shattered the window glass, and struck the assassin's chest. Queen Gwen, Merlin, Gaius, and the Knights could hear the assassin cry in pain as he fell from the palace's wall to the ground.

Caradoc was surrounded by the castle's guards with swords and spears. The assassin was surrounded, and even the windows were filled with soldiers aiming their arrows at the assassin. The palace's emergency bell rang, alerting more guards to a security breach. Queen Gwen, Merlin, Gaius, and the Knights got to the castle's ground floor to find the assassin wounded but still willing to fight.

Queen Gwen asks the assassin, "Why are you risking your life trying to kill the Prince?" "It was my first missed since I started killing many years ago. I'm on a revenge mission to revenge the burning of Queen Viviane by your late King Uther Pendragon. Killing the Queen instead of the Prince means nothing to me. All I wanted is to kill you (Queen Gwen) or the Prince and even a thousand royal guards can't stop me." Replied Caradoc.

Just then, Sir Leon and Sir Percival, along with the rest of the soldiers, arrived at the scene where Caradoc was being surrounded. Sir Leon said, "Caradoc, you aren't going to get away this time." Caradoc looked at Sir Leon and said, "So you know my name?" Sir Percival replied to Caradoc, "You're the greatest assassin from the north. We found the weapon that you used in shooting the young boy in your room. We also discovered that you paid the man at the inn heavily so that you could get a place to shoot directly at your targets. It might interest you that we now have the money paid to you to assassinate the Prince."

This angered Caradoc, who began to fight the guards without fear of being surrounded. Caradoc specialized in using his short size to cut the soldiers' legs before hitting them on their chests with his blade.

As a result, the royal guards were afraid of Caradoc. Caradoc said, "I once killed a hundred guards before killing the Saxon's King. This is something that your Knights would never tell you."

Sir Leon ordered the withdrawal of the foot soldiers to enable the experienced Knights to fight Caradoc. Prince Arthur came down steps to see the man who was trying to assassinate him. Then, Caradoc also uses his blade to cut part of Sir

Leon's skin on his legs. Sir Percival quickly dragged Sir Leon away before Caradoc's blade reached Sir Leon's chest.

A picture of Caradoc fighting Camelot's soldiers after falling from the palace's wall. The Knights and Royal guards could see the assassin sent to kill Prince Arthur.

Caradoc started laughing when he noticed that most of the royal guards were afraid of him. Then Prince Arthur picked up 'The Kings' Sword, which he threw at Caradoc when he climbed up to the castle's wall.

Caradoc said, "Here comes Prince Arthur. I'll surrender after killing you." Caradoc's moves using his short sizes didn't work this time when he was fighting Prince Arthur. He grew angrier and decided to change his fighting tactics. This is something Caradoc hadn't done for a long time. Caradoc raised his body high enough to attack Prince Arthur. Prince Arthur quickly struck Caradoc from behind (Caradoc's back), and the remaining part of Arthur's blade can be seen on Caradoc's front.

Caradoc fell and looked at Prince Arthur, saying, "You aren't an ordinary Prince. There must be a powerful magic working with you." Caradoc died after saying these words. The news that Prince Arthur had killed the notorious assassin spread again like wildfire throughout Camelot and beyond. The news delighted the minds of the people of Camelot as they felt secure because of Prince Arthur's bravery.

CHAPTER SIX

THE KINGS' SWORD DISAPPEARANCE: THE TRIALS OF THE SWORD'S THIEF

In the middle of the night, two men, Palo and Kay, were having a discussing in a forest near the Isle of the Blessed. Kay said to Palo, "Why did you bring me to this horrible and creepy place? We passed through countless skeletons and dead bodies just to get this horrible and creepy place. There isn't anybody to steal from here. I can only see frightening monsters waiting to attack and eat us if we get closer to the castle at the Isle of the Blessed." Palo said to Kay, "You're wrong, Kay; this place was once the greatest magical location where Kings and Queens met with the powerful sorcerers, witches and wizards."

A picture showing Palo and Kay during the dark in a forest near the Isle of the Blessed. They came to steal treasures hidden inside a room at the Isle of the Blessed.

Palo continues, "Guess what the Kings and Queens bring with them when they visit? They will bring gold, silver and other expensive gifts to this place. This place is a treasure house for powerful sorcerers, witches and wizards. We are here to find those gold chests. According to legends, the great sorceress (Nimueh) used to be the richest sorceress who lived in this castle." Kay disagreed with Palo, saying, "I'm going home. You're free to continue with this risky mission."

Kay left Palo alone in the forest and went back home as fast as he could. Palo went closer to the castle on the Isle of the Blessed. Palo brought out an old black pot and recited some magical incarnations. Red smoke came out from the pot and filled everywhere in the Isle of the Blessed. Thus, changing the usual dark color of the Isle of the Blessed into red. It caused Morgana Pendragon and her Wyverns' monsters to fall asleep.

Palo entered the castle on the Isle of the Blessed and went to the center called the 'Serpent Skulls,' where the great sorceress (Nimueh) usually received high dignitaries when she was alive. Palo came to a wall with three giant Serpent Skull heads (This is why people who know this place called it the Serpent Skulls). The Serpent Skulls have frightening eyes that look real. The eyes on the Serpent Skull look real because they see every person who enters the place. Legends had it that Nimueh transformed the three Serpents into stones because they refused to obey her commands.

Palo went to the middle Serpent Skull and recited some magical spells, and the wall opened like a wooden door. Palo was amazed to see various gifts that the late Nimueh had hidden for herself. The huge room contained countless gold chests and diamond chests, which were very rare during Queen Gwen's reign.

As a result, Palo became lost in his greed and forgot that the pot with powerful sleeping smoke clouds wouldn't last long. He was still deliberating on what to carry even though he had already carried five golden chests to the place Kay left him in the forest.

When Morgana Pendragon woke up on her chair beside a fireplace, she didn't feel the presence of a thief. Morgana Pendragon got up from her chair because of a strange light from the center of the 'Serpent Skulls,' which she had never seen before. Morgana Pendragon noticed that someone had opened the door to Nimueh's treasures but couldn't see anyone.

Not quite long, Morgana Pendragon hears

footsteps of someone coming, and she hides herself. Palo has just come back the fifth time to steal more gold and diamonds because he wasn't satisfied with what he got. Just then, Morgana Pendragon steps out of her hiding place. Palo became afraid and wanted to escape. Morgana Pendragon told Palo, "If you try to run, I'll order my monster to have you for breakfast. So, you're the one stealing from me?" Palo replied to Morgana Pendragon, "This is just my first time. It will never happen again."

Morgana Pendragon said, "You're very brave and capable of stealing anything from anyone. I'll let you go on one condition." Palo begged Morgana Pendragon to tell him what she wanted, as he was ready to do it in order to save his life. "I want you to steal 'The Kings' Sword' from the Prince of Camelot and bring the sword to me." Palo happily said, "I'll do it." Palo was about to leave Morgana's presence when she called him to come closer.

Morgana Pendragon said, "Give me your hand." She spat out a small serpent onto Palo's right hand. Palo started crying and pleading that Morgana shouldn't hurt him and that he would do Morgana's bidding. Morgana recites some magic words, and the serpent changes into a golden hand bracelet. Morgana Pendragon says, "If you try to escape without coming back with the sword after seven days, then this snake will strike you dead. You can also tell the snake to kill anyone who prevents you from stealing 'The Kings' Sword' as well.

Palo took a wagon and left the Isle of the Blessed with his gold chests. He was unhappy because of Morgana Pendragon's snake monitor on his hand. Bandits traced Palo because they suspected that he might be carrying some valuable items. The bandits' leader ordered Palo to stop so that they could check if he was carrying some valuable goods.

Palo was just singing without listening to the bandits' leader's order to stop. Palo sang his sorrowful song, saying, "He started hurting for gold at the age of 10 and later found gold at the age of 45 with a snake tied to his hands." The bandits' leader ordered his men to shoot at Palo. One of the arrows fired at Palo struck the snake's bracelet given to Palo by Morgana Pendragon. Then a big snake emerged and started attacking the bandits, who ran for their lives while the unfortunate ones died. Palo felt unconcerned about what was going on. He was singing and riding his wagon towards Camelot.

The great dragon summoned Merlin in the middle of the night. Merlin could hear the dragon calling him. Merlin traced the dragon's call to a nearby wood. The great dragon says to Merlin, "I'm sorry for calling you at this time of the night. I'm just afraid that the Young Prince is about the greatest mistake of his life."

Merlin told the old dragon that he didn't understand what the old dragon was trying to say. Merlin told the old dragon to give him the full details so that he could understand.

The old dragon said, "I received a terrible vision that the Young Prince is about to abandon 'The Kings' Sword' for his own combative skills. This is dangerous for the Prince because "The Kings' Sword' is a jealous weapon. The Prince must always keep the sword with him even when he doesn't intend to use it. Merlin promised the old dragon that the Prince would never abandon 'The Kings' Sword for his own personal skills before returning to the place.

In the morning, Gaius and Merlin, along with other Knights, were summoned to Queen Gwen for an emergency meeting. Queen Gwen remained standing as a knight on guard at the border shared his terrible encounter with a stranger on a wagon headed for Camelot.

The Knight told the Queen Gwen. I was at a guard on the border between Albion and the Kingdom of Cornwall when my men and I noticed a lonely rider on a wagon riding towards Camelot. We stopped the stranger on the wagon for inspection, but he didn't respond to our commands.

Therefore, we decided to use force. Surprisingly, a gigantic snake from his hand's bracelet attacked us. Many of my men are wounded as I speak. I came to inform you that the man with the evil bracelet might enter Camelot if he isn't stopped.

Queen Gwen ordered two of her trusted and bravest Knights, Sir Leon and Sir Percival, to prevent the strange man and his wagon from entering Camelot. Sir Leon and Sir Percival assembled some soldiers and left immediately.

Palo stops at a village near Camelot to see his family. He tells his wife to share the treasures among his children if he doesn't come home again because he is on a dangerous mission. Palo tells his wife not to cry, but he must carry out the mission given to him by a powerful witch. Palo continues his journey on a horse.

Palo was singing on his horse when Sir Leon and Sir Percival passed by searching for a man on a wagon. They didn't know that the man they were looking for was now riding a horse.

Merlin was fetching roots for Gaius' medicine when he noticed a man on a horse looking at the castle. Merlin greeted the man (Palo), but he didn't reply to Merlin's greeting. Merlin saw a strange bracelet with a terrible snake head. Merlin thought that meeting with Queen Gwen was about the man on the wagon carrying a dangerous snake's bracelet. He became confused because the man he saw was on a horse instead of a wagon.

Merlin asks Gaius, "Does the Knight say the man with the snake bracelet was riding a wagon and not a horse?" Gaius didn't reply to Merlin because Merlin had brought the ingredients for the Queen's medicine late.

As a result, Gaius was hurrying to prepare the medicine so that the Queen could take her medicine on time. Thus, Gaius doesn't have time to answer Merlin's questions, so Merlin goes to bed.

Prince Arthur couldn't sleep, so he went to the training ground to practice at night. He didn't go with his sword. The night guards were busy watching Prince Arthur trains alone, and they didn't know when Palo entered the castle through the window.

Prince Arthur's sword disappears immediately. Palo came close to Prince Arthur's room. Then, 'The Kings' Sword vanished. The disappearance of 'The Kings' Sword' shattered the glasses of Prince

Arthur's windows where the Prince kept his sword. The old dragon became angry about the disappearance of 'The Kings' Sword because he (the old dragon) felt that the sword had disappeared. Also, Prince Arthur became suspicious that something was wrong in his room because of the broken glasses in his windows. Prince Arthur returns to his room to find that his sword is missing.

Camelot's emergency bell began ringing to alert the guards to the sudden disappearance of the sword. The bell woke Merlin, and he discovered that Gaius wasn't in his room. Because of the missing sword, Merlin finds Queen Gwen, Gaius, and Prince Arthur in Prince Arthur's room. This was when Merlin remembered that the old dragon had warmed him regarding the sword. Gaius informed Merlin that Prince Arthur's sword was missing.

Merlin left Queen Gwen's castle and went straight into the woods to meet the great dragon who was already waiting for Merlin. Merlin told the old dragon, "The Kings' Sword has gone missing. I'm afraid someone has stolen the Prince's sword." The old dragon says, "No one is capable of carrying 'The King's Sword' except its bearer, as it is too heavy for anyone who isn't the wielder to lift the sword."

Merlin says, "This means there is a possibility that the sword might still be in Prince Arthur's room." "Precisely!" Replied the old dragon. "I can still feel the presence of 'The King's sword' in Prince Arthur's room. The reason for the sword's invisibility to Prince Arthur might be that it is angry, or someone is trying to steal it." Said the old dragon.

Merlin told the old dragon, "Prince Arthur being at the training ground without the sword in his hand might have triggered its disappearance." The old dragon says, "He guessed that there I someone in the Queen's palace with an evil mission for the Prince's sword. Until this person is found. The sword would continue to remain invisible."

Merlin returned to the castle. He transformed into Emrys and went to Prince Arthur's room. Queen Gwen was pleased to see him. Emrys told the Queen and Prince Arthur that the sword was hiding because someone wanted to steal it. Just then, Emrys suspects a man guarding one of the rooms. This is because Emrys could hear the hisses of the snake bracelet on his hand. The snake even eyed Emrys. A hand bracelet is something that royal guards don't put on their hands. Thus, this is a clear sign that the guard (Palo) guarding the room is a false guard.

Prince Arthur summons the captain of the royal

guard to identify the suspected man. Palo sees that the captain is approaching him and starts to run. The captain orders Palo to stop, but he refuses and jumps out of the window.

Palo died after jumping from an upstairs room in the castle to the ground. Then, the snake in his bracelet emerged and started to attack the royal guards. Emrys quickly went down to find a giant snake. Emrys recites a magical spell and changes the snake to stone. The snake, now turned to stone, fell and shattered into pieces.

Prince Arthur could see the sudden appearance of 'The Kings' Sword after Palo had been declared dead. Emrys explained to Queen Gwen and Prince Arthur that the sword's disappearance was an act of self-preservation to protect itself from Palo, who was attempting to steal it.

CHAPTER SEVEN

THE NIGHT FOR NIGHTJAR'S EVIL MISSION

After Palo's theft, Morgana Pendragon continued searching for evil magical items in the Serpents Skulls' room, which enabled her to find hidden magical items. Morgana Pendragon found a huge black bird in a bottle. The name of the gigantic bird in the bottle was Nightjar.

Nightjar could identify Morgana Pendragon's name and called her the priestess of the old region. This makes Morgana Pendragon develop her interest in such an evil bird. Nightjar says, "I could spy on your enemies and even deliver deadly portions into the food of your foes whenever you order."

Morgana Pendragon laughs, saying, "You see, Nightjar, most of my endeavors to kill my step brother usually fails. This is because the people I sent to each mission usually fail to carry on the mission as planned." "I could poison the Prince Arthur if that would make you happy." Said Nightjar to Morgana Pendragon. Morgana Pendragon says to Nightjar, "I've no poisonous portion at this moment." "I could help you search for one from among Nimueh's magical treasures." Requested Nightjar.

Morgana Pendragon broke the bottle to release the Nightjar. There was black smoke and thunder and lightning that came from the broken bottle before the appearance of Nightjar. Nightjar stood in front of Morgana Pendragon and bowed down as a sign of showing his loyalty to Morgana Pendragon.

Morgana Pendragon says within herself, "That sending Nightjar on a mission to poison Queen Gwen wasn't her main assignment for Nightjar. I just want Nightjar to proves himself worth to become my trusted pet."

A dark room featuring Morgana Pendragon in the Serpents Skulls' room where she evil magical items, including a bottle containing a trapped magical bird named Nightjar.

Morgana Pendragon abandoned Nightjar to search for the poison itself. Soon, Nightjar arrives with a bottle with a liquid content that looks reddish in color. Morgana couldn't believe Nightjar's instincts. Her original plan was to find where Nimueh had hidden the vest containing the dead witches and wizards' powers, which could make her more powerful and help her kill Merlin and her enemies. This was Morgana Pendragon's optimal goal.

Morgana Pendragon told Nightjar, "Your first task is to poison Queen Gwen of Camelot. Return when you've completed this mission. Then you would become my trusted pet." Nightjar bows down to Morgana Pendragon before embarking on his journey to Camelot.

Gaius and Merlin were busy arguing about which food was more delicious in their room. Gaius told Merlin, saying, "I can cook better than all the Queen Gwen's cooks. Gaius angrily left Queen Gwen's quarters because Merlin disagreed with him, saying that the palace's cooks cooked better than Gaius. Merlin then poured Gaius' food into a plate for the birds to eat. This is something that Merlin does anytime he doesn't feel like eating Gaius' food.

Then came the Nightjar, who came to eat the food with other birds that Merlin had just poured into the plate near his window. Merlin overheard Nightjar communicating with other birds using the Druid's language, which non-Druids couldn't understand. The Nightjar began driving away other birds, pecking at them dangerously and even killing three. Merlin has never seen such a bird or any bird displayed in such a dangerous manner.

In the middle of the night, Merlin woke up. He couldn't sleep. Merlin was afraid to sleep because he continued to see the same dream repeatedly. This is something that Merlin has never experienced before in his life. Merlin decided to visit his old dragon friend to share the frightening nightmare that prevented him from sleeping. "Why do you summon me at this time of the night, young warlock?" Asked the old dragon.

"I saw a gigantic bird eating the corpses of Prince Arthur and Queen Gwen including other Knights. Then the bird turns toward me, wanting to eat my corpse." Said Merlin. The old dragon asked Merlin further, saying, "Do you mean a frightening black bird eating the corpses of Prince Arthur and Queen Gwen, the Knights, and your friend Gaius on the palace's dining table?" Merlin was surprised that the old dragon shared the same dream with him.

"Are you having the same dream, or you saw it in

your vision?" Asked Merlin. "Merlin, you and I share the same magical bond. "I always see anything that you see and sometimes hear any words that you listen to. The dream is a terrible warming because there is a possibility that you might neglect such warming from your dream. That is why you keep having the nightmare repeatedly." Replied the old dragon. Merlin looks surprised because he feels that his friends are in great danger.

"The bird you saw in your dream is called the Nightjar. Nightjar is a rare bird because it was produced by magic. It is a curse to speak of such a bird in the daytime. It is eviler to see such a bird in one sleep because the Nightjar can appear in front of the dreamer to kill in real life," Said the old dragon. Merlin asked the old dragon, saying, "To kill the dreamer?" "Precisely," Replied the old dragon.

"What can be done to avert the coming evils from the Nightjar?" Asked Merlin. The old dragon continues his talking to Merlin saying, "The old dragon continues talking to Merlin, saying, "The Nightjar must return to the bottle from where it came. That is when the Nightjar would never hurt any person either in the dream or in a real-life situation."

"How would I defeat the Nightjar?" Asked Merlin.

The old dragon says, "You ask the wrong question, Merlin." Merlin asks the old dragon, saying, "What is the right question?" "We should ask ourselves who released the Nightjar, and what is the Nightjar's mission in Camelot?" Answered the old dragon.

Merlin replied to the old dragon, saying, "Who is capable of releasing the Nightjar?" The old dragon answered, "Only the priestesses of the old region are capable of summoning the Nightjar." "Morgana Pendragon is the current priestess of the old region, which means she summoned the Nightjar to harm my friends." Merlin replied.

Merlin recited some magical transformation spells, and he changed into Emrys. He normally does this when there are some important magic tasks to be done.

Queen Gwen was at her window when she saw Emrys entering the castle. Queen Gwen went to meet Emrys, saying, "What brings you to Camelot at this time?" Emrys told Queen Gwen, saying, "Morgana Pendragon has released an evil bird known as the Nightjar."

Queen Gwen said, "I heard the laughing of a strange black bird by my window. The bird flew away when it saw me coming approaching with a broom stick." As Emrys was about to check to see if the Nightjar was still standing near Queen Gwen's window, Emrys and Queen Gwen could hear the footsteps of soldiers marching towards them.

Emrys and Queen Gwen quietly looked in the direction of the marching soldiers' footsteps. They found that the marching soldiers had eagle heads while the rest of their bodies were human.

Queen Gwen asked Emrys, saying, "Who are these?" Emrys replies to Queen Gwen, saying, "They're the royal guards under the influence of the Nightjar." "They're getting closer. What are we going to do?" Asked Queen Gwen.

Emrys looked up and saw a huge Camelot's flag. Emrys used the magic in his eyes, which makes the big Camelot's flag to fall on the soldiers with eagle heads and half-humans. Emrys told Queen that he didn't want to hurt the soldiers because they would change back to their original form once the evil bird is captured.

Emrys and Queen Gwen went to Gaius' room to tell him about the Nightjar. On getting there, they found that the Nightjar had already turned Gaius into a half-horse and half-human creature known as a centaur. The centaur's face looked exactly like Gaius', but the remaining half of his body was that of a horse. The centaur started chasing Emrys and

Queen Gwen. Emrys has to lock Gaius (who has transformed into a centaur) inside his room to prevent him from hurting other people living in the castle.

Queen Gwen asked Emrys, "Who turned Gaius into a centaur?" I guessed it is the Nightjar bird from Morgana Pendragon." Just then, the Nightjar appeared to Queen Gwen and Emrys, saying, "Someone calling my name. Someone who wants to sleep is calling my name." Immediately, Queen Gwen started feeling sleepy.

Emrys remembered the warmings from the great dragon saying, "Those who fall asleep whenever the Nightjar sings will see evil things in their dreams. They will eventually even be transformed into whatever creatures they see in their dreams."

Emrys quickly poured water on Queen Gwen's face, saying, "Please, stay awake because we need to fight and capture this evil before sunrise. Only then we could undo all the evils that the Nightjar has done this night." Queen Gwen, who has just been revived by the water poured on her face, promised Emrys to remain awake until the Nightjar bird is captured.

Emrys pointed his finger towards the Nightjar, and fire came from his hand, which struck the Nightjar, but the Nightjar flew before Emrys' fire could reach the window where it was singing.

Emrys and Queen Gwen could hear the Nightjar singing. Queen Gwen told Emrys, saying, "Nightjar's voice is coming from Prince Arthur's room. My son could be in danger." Emrys says to Queen Gwen, "We must be careful not to hurt the Prince. We must search for a way to undo all these evils caused by Nightjar."

Queen Gwen and Emrys traced Nightjar's voice to Prince Arthur's room. Emrys, followed by Queen Gwen, opens Prince Arthur's room door quietly to find that the Nightjar has turned Prince Arthur into a questing beast creature. A questing monster is a creature with the head of a serpent, the body of a leopard, the haunches of a lion, and the feet of a deer. The beast started chasing Queen Gwen and Emrys. It was about to eat Queen Gwen's hand when Emrys pushed the hungry creature back into Prince Arthur's room with a strong wind from his hands.

Emrys now holds Queen Gwen's hands, saying, "That monster isn't your son. Prince Arthur isn't a questing monster. We must look for a way to undo all these evils magic in the castle before the sun rises."

Queen Gwen started crying at her son's sudden appearance. My Queen, your cries won't solve any problem. It would make things worse. We need a plan to capture the evil bird alive in a bottle."

Queen Gwen said, "The whole palace's creatures are against us. We're just two persons. Everyone has turned into evil beings. I'm afraid, Emrys, there isn't anything we can do." "There is something we can do, my Queen. We need to trace the Nightjar to where it is calling us and capture it," said Emrys.

Just then, they heard Prince Arthur calling Queen Gwen. The Nightjar was also whispering, saying, "Your son is calling you, my Queen." Emrys says to Queen Gwen, "You must go in first and pretend to obey everything the Nightjar tells you, and I'll capture the Nightjar from behind."

Queen Gwen agreed with Emrys' plan to capture the Nightjar. She traced Prince Arthur's voice to the dining table, where he was sitting with two glasses filled with something that looked like blood. Prince Arthur told the Queen to sit down so that they could have a drink.

The Nightjar stood at the dining table, and Queen Gwen could clearly see the evil bird's eyes. Queen Gwen sat beside the questing beast creature, which her son turned into on the dining table. The Nightjar continued to look into Queen Gwen's eyes to figure out her plans with Emrys.

Just before the Nightjar is about to figure out Queen Gwen's plan from reading her eyes when Emrys, appears behind the Nightjar with a large bottle. The Nightjar flies inside the bottle unknowingly. The bottle was the same bottle broken by Morgana Pendragon. Emrys has just returned from the Isle of the Blessed with the mended bottle, which the bottle's magic pulled the Nightjar back to where it belongs.

Prince Arthur, who is now a questing beast, wants to attack Emrys and Queen Gwen, but Emrys recites a magical word, and a spider web covers the creature. Emrys quickly took Queen Gwen to her room and asked her to lock the door.

Emrys told Queen Gwen, "I'm going to take the captured Nightjar (now in a bottle) back to the pool of Nemhain. The pool of Nemhain is a veil between the world of the living and the death. Everything would return to their original forms once I dropped the bottle with the Nightjar inside."

Queen Gwen kissed Emrys, "Saying good luck, my friend." Emrys warmed Queen Gwen not to open the door until the sun rose, as the Nightjar's spells were still active. Emrys closed the door and left for Nemhain's pool.

Queen Gwen suddenly heard all the evil creatures

knocking on her door very hard. She shouted, but no one came to her rescue. Suddenly, her door broke. All the creatures, including the soldiers with eagle heads, the centaur, the questing monster, and other frightening beings, started getting closer to her.

Just then, the sun rose with its powerful rays, shinning on all the evil creatures. This caused the evil creatures to walk backward to where they were before the Nightjar changed them into monsters. When they got to where they were before, the evil creatures changed back to their original human forms.

Some creatures with eagle heads and human bodies change back to human forms (royal guards) when they get to the palace's gates. Gaius was changed back from a centaur creature into a human. Prince Arthur changed from a questing beast back into a human and was now sleeping in his bed. So goes everything that Nightjar has transformed.

Emrys was seen standing at Nemhain's pool and smiling at the sun. He watched the sun's rays touch everything in Camelot, changing them back to their original forms.

END OF THE SECOND SERIES

Dear Readers,

We wanted to extend our heartfelt thanks for choosing to embark on the magical journey of "The Return of Merlin" series with us by purchasing the first book. We hope you've enjoyed the enchanting world of King Arthur, Merlin, and Morgana Pendragon in this second series. Kindly get the first series if you've not read it.

Your support and enthusiasm mean the world to us, and we're thrilled to have you as a part of our literary adventure. The story has only just begun, and more epic adventures, twists, and turns are waiting in the upcoming series.

We invite you to continue this extraordinary adventure with us in the next series of "The Return of Merlin." Discover more secrets, unravel ancient prophecies, and join our beloved characters in their quest for destiny. The magic, mystery, and adventure are far from over.

Thank you for being a part of "The Return of Merlin" family. We look forward to your continued support and hope you'll accompany us on this remarkable path as the story unfolds. Kindly give a positive review if you find this book fascinating.

Warm regards

ABOUT THE AUTHOR

Richard Bernard is an author. He has written other books at Kindle Publishing. He has been a co-writer of many seasonal novels, including academic journals, for over fifteen years.

Printed in Great Britain
by Amazon